I0788112

MAD MAX
&
SWEET SARAH

MAD MAX
&
SWEET SARAH

Ellie Collins

Fresh Ink Group
Guntersville

Mad Max & Sweet Sarah

Fresh Ink Group
An Imprint of:
The Fresh Ink Group, LLC
1021 Blount Avenue, #931
Guntersville, AL 35976
Email: info@FreshInkGroup.com
FreshInkGroup.com

Edition 1.0   2020

Cover design by Matthew Collins
Book design by Amit Dey / FIG
Associate publisher Lauren A. Smith / FIG

Cataloging-in-Publication Recommendations:
YAF011000 YOUNG ADULT FICTION / Coming of Age
YAF019010 YOUNG ADULT FICTION / Fantasy / Contemporary
YAF038000 YOUNG ADULT FICTION / Magical Realism

Library of Congress Control Number: 2019919570

ISBN-13: 978-1-947867-72-7 Papercover
ISBN-13: 978-1-947867-71-0 Hardcover
ISBN-13: 978-1-947867-75-8 Ebooks

Mad Max
&
Sweet Sarah

Chapter I

Max

"Ladies and gentlemen, Hawaiian Airlines welcomes you to Seattle, Washington. The local time is 8:53 p.m.."

There really was no turning back now. It had felt so surreal, seeing the lights of the Space Needle, Big Wheel, and pro-sports stadiums shining below him as they made their descent. Now Max's hands broke out in a cold sweat and his breath seemed to catch in his throat as the reality of where he was and where he was going hit him like a rogue wave to the face.

The plane slowly rolled forward toward their gate. Passengers around him were whipping out cell phones, checking emails, and texting loved ones. He wouldn't be texting anyone. The people he loved were all back on O'ahu. . .where he belonged. "Just two weeks. Just two weeks," he chanted under his breath, trying to shake off the panic closing in around him.

A chorus of clicking seatbelts, rapidly rising voices, and pops of the opening overhead bins filled the cabin as people stood, stretched, and retrieved their carry-on luggage. Max didn't move from his seat. He convinced himself he was just being considerate to travelers who were in a hurry. Maybe some had connecting flights with little time to get to their next gate. Who was he to prevent them from making their next plane on time?

All too soon, though, the last passenger passed by and there were no excuses left. Snapping off his seatbelt, he slowly grabbed his backpack from under the seat in front of him, stood, slung it over his shoulder, and carefully removed his duffle bag from the already opened overhead bin.

"Mahalo! Enjoy your stay," the flight attendant murmured through her tired-looking fake smile as he approached the door. She didn't want to be here right now any more than he did. She probably longed for the beaches of home, too.

Max weaved his way through a group of waiting passengers, then set his bags down so he could swing the hood of his sweatshirt up over his head. Makuahine was right; it was cooler here than back home. Grabbing his bags with a heavy sigh, he set out, following signs to the baggage-claim area where his ride was supposed to be waiting. His steps slowed, the closer he got to his destination. His mouth dried out. His brow sweat. His heart pounded.

Stop it! he scolded himself. *There's no reason to be nervous!*

"Maddox?" A deep voice from behind interrupted his thoughts.

Max stopped. *Already? I thought I'd have a minute or two more to prepare for this!* He turned slowly.

The man before him was taller than expected—two or three inches taller than Max. Hints of gray mixed with the short chestnut hair and carefully trimmed beard he recognized from the pictures. He wore khaki pants, brown loafers, and a light blue dress shirt with the sleeves rolled up to his elbows. So, this was him.

This was his father.

Why was it, again, that Max had never met this man once in all his sixteen years? It had never seemed all that important back home, but now the question burned within him, hot and all-consuming. How is it he and Makuahine had never really talked much about it? Was his mother trying to protect him from being hurt by his father's abandonment? Had Max been a disappointment to him? Would he be a disappointment now? Here was an opportunity to get to know each other, but what if he was rejected. . .again?

Then anger washed over Max. It was an unfamiliar and uncomfortable feeling, but he grabbed onto it and clung desperately to the overwhelming emotion that effectively drowned out all his confusion, uncertainty, and insecurity.

He wasn't sure why, but Max didn't want to let his until-now absent parent know he was so affected by this meeting. If his father wanted that level of communication and intimacy, he should have earned it. Long ago. Right?

Mustering the most bored, irritated tone he could, he responded, "Yeah?" He hoped none of his underlying panic bled through his "attitude problem" disguise.

"Hi!" Max was greeted with a tight smile, but thankfully no attempts at physical contact like a handshake or—God forbid—a hug. "I was beginning to think you missed your flight or got lost in the airport or something. The board said your plane landed twenty-five minutes ago."

Max didn't know what excuse for his delay would be most believable. He considered an honest approach, something like, *No, I just didn't want to be here,* but he decided to go with a less confrontational shoulder shrug.

"Then I, uh, . . . almost didn't recognize you." Awkward chuckle. "Has—. . . has your hair been that color for long?"

Max was definitely picking up an uneasy vibe from his father. Part of him reveled in the fact that he wasn't the only one feeling uncomfortable, but the rest of him almost felt bad. Almost. He wasn't ready to diffuse the situation with idol chit-chat, though. It felt like that would be too generous. "No," he answered simply, in a flat tone.

Cool blue eyes appraised Max with a raised brow. Was this man—this *stranger*—waiting for further explanation? Too bad—he'd be waiting a long time. Seeming to get that message from Max's carefully executed blank stare, the man offered a grim nod of acceptance and began walking toward the escalator, indicating that Max should follow with a sweeping motion of his left arm. "Yeah. Okay. Well, then. . .I'm sure you're tired after a long day of travel. Let's get you home, shall we?"

Home? He's gotta be kidding. I have no home here. Still, Max had promised he'd give this little charade two weeks and he would stay true to his word. With a sigh, he fell in step behind his father. Or his dad. That's probably how he should refer to him, right? But it didn't feel right. . .*at all.* He'd just stick with David for now.

It was trippy to think that the man walking in front of him was responsible for half of the genes in his body. He wondered what that meant. Did they have random things in common—little quirks with no other explanation, like his hate for cilantro, aptitude in math, and nail-biting habit? They didn't appear to have fashion sense in common, that was for sure.

The pair silently made their way through the parking garage. His father pulled a key fob out of his pocket and pushed a button. A nearby car's lights flashed and made a chirping sound. *A Beamer. Pff. Figures.* The trunk popped open before they reached the car. Max threw his bags in, closed the trunk, and hopped in the back seat where he could pretend this was just an awkward Uber ride or something. The front seat would be too close and would encourage conversation.

In the forty-five minutes or so to Kirkland, Washington, David attempted exactly three questions: *Is the temperature of the car okay? Do you want the radio on or off?* And: *How was school this year?*

Max prided himself on his single syllable answers. "Yep." "On." "Fine."

He coupled his last answer with a sigh and made sure his eye roll could be heard in his tone, since he doubted his father could see him through the rearview mirror in the darkened car. He definitely couldn't handle any type of father-son heart-to-heart. He was struggling just to wrap his head around everything. He wanted to avoid any other open-ended questions.

It worked. The questions ceased. They were left with only the '80s *Hottest Hits* assaulting them through the car's high-end sound system. For real—'80s! Clearly they didn't share taste in music. He should have answered "Off" to that second question. He didn't want to run the risk of David thinking he was trying to drum up more conversation, though, so he suffered through the noise.

Luckily, the journey ended before "Wake Me Up Before You Go-Go" by Wham! had gotten to the second verse. Be thankful for small favors; isn't that what Makuahine always told him? They entered a massive three-car garage attached to a massive house. They parked next to a massive Land Rover. He wondered just how much more bizarre this little adventure could possibly get.

Max grabbed his bags out of the trunk and followed his father through a door into the kitchen of the house. That's when bizarre escalated to insanity. It began with a high-pitched screeching sound and a huge punch to his gut that nearly knocked him off his feet.

No, wait. Not a punch. A hug. He looked down to find a blond head attached to his chest.

Before he could process what was going on, the owner of the blond hair pulled away and yelled over her shoulder. "Diva! Come here! Come meet your Uncle Maddox!"

Then the most ridiculous creature Max had ever seen flew around the corner at a dizzying speed. It was some sort of a miniature, white, poofy dog-type animal—wearing a tutu? And, son of a biscuit, . . . a tiara?

"Maddox, this is Cupcake Diva—Diva for short. Div, this is Uncle Maddox! But wait, that feels so *formal.* Uncle Mad? Maddie? No—that's a girl name. What should we call him?" the hug ambusher addressed the doggish being, apparently expecting a response.

"Max," he was finally able to spit out, recovering from his stunned silence. "Everyone who knows me just calls me Max." He shot David a pointed look, calling his father out on not knowing him enough to know what name he goes by.

"Ooo. . .I have it then! You'll be my Maxie! You don't mind if I call you Maxie, right? It's *perfect!*" she declared as she pulled away to arm's length. "Now, let me get a good look at my handsome big brother! Wow. . .look at your skin! It's so tan! It's like caramel. Yummy! Mine's just bland and pasty white; I can't stay outside for more than, like, ten minutes without turning red as a lobster," she declared, snorting out a laugh. "But you. . ." she continued in an awed tone, "you look like you just walked off a tropical sandy beach!"

"I kinda did. . ." Max commented, although it was wasted because this chick was on a roll and wasn't hearing a thing.

"And your clothes are so cool, too! You've totally got the whole beach vibe *down*, with your board shorts and flip-flops." She interrupted her speech with a dramatic gasp as she looked down at herself. "Oh, how cool would it have been if I met you while wearing a matching outfit! But. . .impossible. Div and I were totally in a tutu mood, and once you find yourself there, you *just* have to go with it—know what I mean?"

"No. . .not really. . ." Max mumbled as he realized with some level of alarm that blondie and the dogette were, indeed, wearing matching outfits. Holy House of Horrors, Batman; he was further out of his element than he ever dreamed. He actually caught himself looking over to David for help.

Again, his comment was bowled right over with running commentary. "Oh, and look at your *hair!*" She was now pulling his hood down for a closer inspection. "Ohmygod, Daddy, I literally want my hair Just. Like. This! It is sooooo cool! It's all business black in the back, but the front is totally *on fiah!*"

Max was feeling a curious mix of awkward, uncomfortable, and. . .flattered. He couldn't remember anyone complimenting his attire before, let alone his skin tone, and he thought his hair was pretty bitchin', too, so he certainly didn't mind being called out on it. He had never dyed his hair before. There'd be no point; the sun and salt-water would bleach it out before he even got to enjoy it. He knew he'd miss his surf and sand terribly over the next two weeks—he'd never been away from it that long before—so his consolation prize to himself was getting his long bangs that hung over his right eye dyed red, orange, and yellow—like flames.

"Can I? Can I? Can I, Daddy?" the wild child continued, yet to have taken a new breath.

"Sarah! Please! Just. . .tone it down for a second, okay?" David had his arms outstretched and pumped them up and down to chill the kid out, but with the way he chuckled and shook his head, no way would anyone take him seriously. "Honey, you need to give Madd—uh, Max—a minute to catch his breath!"

"I knoooow, but I'm just so *excited!* You know I've been begging you to get Maxie here for, like, six or eight or a bajillian months now!" Sarah smiled angelically up at Max. "I just couldn't go on another day without getting to know my big brother! And now I have you! For the whole summer!" She started excitedly bouncing up and down on her toes.

"Wait—" All of Max's good humor left in a gush. "All summer?" he demanded from David. "I thought you said I only had to stay here for two weeks?"

"Well, you were pretty adamant about the two-week trial period, but as I said on the phone, I'm sure you'll love it here for the summer!" David smiled as he said this, but it didn't quite reach his eyes. He appeared just as unsure about Max loving his time in Washington as Max was positive he'd be back on a plane in exactly thirteen days, six hours, and counting.

David nervously cleared his throat. "As a matter of fact," he continued, "I was even able to snag you a lifeguard position at our neighborhood pool. Your mom mentioned that you have a lifeguarding license. I figured it would give you a little extra spending money, and it'd be a great way to meet other kids your age while you're here."

"Wait. What? You got me a *job?* But. . .you said *two weeks!*" Max's voice cracked embarrassingly on the final two words of that sentence, his throat feeling like it was closing up on him as panic took hold again.

David seemed to pick up on his distress. "You know what? It's all okay. If it doesn't work out, it doesn't work out. Let's just get some rest and we can start fresh in the morning."

"Yeah, Maxie, you're gonna *love* it here. Trust me. I'm gonna make sure you have the Time. Of. Your *LIFE!*" Sarah declared, clapping with each word for emphasis.

Nothing about this felt anything like the time of Max's life.

CHAPTER II

Max

With Diva tucked into a ridiculous over-the-shoulder pouch, Sarah gave Max a quick tour of the house before they turned in for the night. The layout was pretty simple, but far removed from anything he could relate to. The minimalist furnishings, surrounded by extensive walls of eggshell white and interrupted by occasional works of abstract art, seemed to add to the cooler temperatures of the Pacific Northwest. He didn't feel like he belonged. He missed the warm and welcoming little home he shared with his mom and grandparents. Pretty much the total opposite of this place, his house was nothing noteworthy to anyone else, but forever special to him. It was roomy enough for everyone, especially since Uncle Josh and Uncle Mike moved out to the house next door. Besides, who cared about the size of the house? They all spent nearly all their time outdoors, anyway.

Around the corner from the kitchen they came to a closed door. Sarah put a finger to her lips, signaling for Max to stay quiet, and silently swung it open to reveal a home office. Behind a big mahogany desk sat a woman with long blond hair that matched Sarah's. She wore a headset and talked while typing on a lap-top, but she shot a beautiful smile in their direction and offered a friendly little wave before Sarah softly closed the door.

"That's my mom—Rebecca," Sarah explained as they moved on to a third living room-type area. "She felt really bad that she wouldn't be able to greet you, but she had another one of her important overseas calls. I think this one was someone in Australia. . .or China. . .I don't know; I lose track. Anyway, she'll be spending the day with us tomorrow, so you'll get a chance to meet her then."

"Spending the day with us?"

"Oh yeah. I have the whole day planned out for you! Daddy has to work, but Mom said she'd be able to take us. She'll have to make a few calls along the way, but she said she wouldn't have to be in the house for those."

"Where are we going?"

"Into Seattle. But that's all I'm telling you; the rest is a surprise!" She giggled and rubbed her hands together with a conspicuously mischievous expression.

Great, Max thought. He shuddered to think what this kid had planned for them. *Just two weeks*, he resumed his silent chant, *just two weeks. . .*

They passed a grandfather clock chiming out the late hour as they wound up a carpeted staircase toward the bedrooms. Sarah led him to the second doorway on the right, proudly informing him that she had taken the liberty of getting a new blue comforter for the queen-sized guest bed because the quilt that had been on it had a pattern that was "entirely too floral for you." He stepped into the spacious room, noticing the comforter, but it was the huge attached bathroom that captured his attention and disbelief. He had never shared a bathroom with fewer than three other people before. Man. . .when he peed on the seat, who could he possibly blame it on? But, . . .if it were his bathroom alone, . . .who would possibly care? *I could get used to this*, he thought as a smirk spread over his face.

Sarah skipped off to her room, leaving Max alone to prepare for bed. He shut the bedroom door and stood for a moment, startled by the silence. No TV blared in the next room, no visiting family members taunting each other playfully over a hand of cards, no singing and laughing around a bonfire outside.

He shivered from the physical chill that oozed from the lonely quiet engulfing him. Unnerved, he grabbed his phone and was about to call home when he stopped, thinking about what he would say to Makuahine when he got her. She had encouraged him to make this trip. If she hadn't, he'd be home right now, soaking in all the sounds so familiar to him. If he called to tell her how much he missed home, how much he wished he never came, she might feel guilty for pushing him into it. He didn't want his mother to feel bad. After hovering his thumb over the call button for a full minute, he sighed and just typed out a text instead.

Max: Hey. Made it safe. Headed to bed. Love you!

Makuahine: Maika'I loa! Aloha'oe, e ke aloha! [Excellent! Love you, too, sweetheart!]

Max grabbed his charger out of his backpack, plugged his phone in, shut off the light, and climbed into bed. The cold of the sheets with the complete lack of light and sound made him think of tombs. He jumped out of bed and threw the light back on. Taking a breath, he padded over to the bathroom, turned the light on, and shut the door halfway. He shut the bedroom light back off and sighed with some relief once he was back in bed. Then he rubbed his hands over his face and groaned, shaking his head. He couldn't imagine the ribbing he'd get from his cousins if they found out he needed a nightlight.

No. He didn't *need* one. It was just so he wouldn't trip over the furniture if he had to go to the bathroom in the middle of the night. That's all. Besides, he'd shut it off before anyone saw it in the morning. Nobody would know.

With that settled, his mind snuck back to the events of the evening. He didn't want to revisit all those recent memories; they were entirely too overwhelming and uncomfortable. He was interested in learning about his father, but wasn't a fan of what he had learned so far: David would take the liberty of getting his son a job without first discussing it with said son, and he. . .also liked '80s music. Max shuddered at the thought. Maybe a lifeguarding job wouldn't be such a bad thing, though. It would get him out of this house during the day, and it would put him near water, where he always felt most comfortable. And he'd be able to save up the money he made for that sweet board he had been checking out at the surf shop. Still, though,. . .David should have talked to him first.

Then there was Sarah. He didn't know *what* the heck to make of that crazy kid. How could he share any DNA with someone who talked so fast and wore a matching tutu with a *dog?* That being said, she had obviously been overjoyed to meet him, which felt good, but apparently she was the very reason he was here at all, and for that he wished she had just minded her own business and kept to her own life.

He tried to shake it all out of his head. He wanted to be done thinking for the night. Great. Now all that left was the chorus to "Wake Me Up Before You Go-Go." No! With a defeated groan he slammed his head under his pillow, trying to escape the offending noise that nobody else could hear.

Sarah

Sarah tucked Diva into bed next to herself and grabbed her phone.

Text from Sarah to Keelie: Hey, you still all good to puppysit tomorrow?

Keelie: Sho nuf! Soooooo. . .is he there? What's he like?

Sarah: OMG, he's awesome, Kee! He's all tall, dark, and broody. And he has this wicked red hair that I TOTALLY want!

Keelie: Wait, RED hair?! I thought his mom is a native Hawaiian!

Sarah: Not natural, silly. It's dyed red, orange, and yellow in the front so it looks like he has flames falling down over the side of his face

Keelie: Ohhh. . .that sounds cool

Sarah: Yeah; he's a real firecracker!

Keelie: Seriously?

Sarah: Come on! Fire. . .firecracker!

Keelie: Even for you that's a pretty pathetic pun.

Sarah: Eh, you're just jealous you didn't think it up first. I'll see you in the AM. Hugs! 🖤

Keelie: Toodles 🖤

Sarah plugged her phone in for the night, grabbed her book from her bedside table, and settled into bed next to Diva with a long satisfied sigh. She had done it. She had gotten her brother here. Sometimes she thought it might not happen, but here he was—right *here*! Now they could be the close, loving family she had imagined for a long time.

Her tired, old daydreams took on new life and color with Maxie actually in the house. She could nearly *feel* them sitting in the living room together on nights when Mom and Dad were working late. They might argue over who got to choose what to watch on Netflix or which video game they'd play, but they'd work it all out and have fun in the end. She could almost *smell* the popcorn they'd munch on together.

Outside of the house, Sarah imagined Maxie would be all standoffish in public, acting like he didn't want to be seen with her, but she got goosebumps imagining the relief, love, and gratitude when he'd get super protective when people called her annoying or stupid.

Having a big brother was going to be *awesome*. Now big bro just needed to decide that having a little sister would be awesome, too. Shaking off her daydream, Sarah focused on what she'd need to do to reach her goal. Maxie was still on the fence about whether or not he wanted to be there. She accepted the challenge and hoped the trip she had planned for tomorrow would go a long way in convincing him this was right where he wanted to be.

Too excited to sleep and inspired by her own situation, she delved into some stories about god and demigod brothers and sisters in the big book of Greek mythology she had snatched up from a second-hand bookstore on the other side of town.

*   *   *

Potential catastrophe number one was avoided. The sky shone a brilliant blue, with no rain in the forecast. Sarah breathed a sigh of relief as she gulped down a bowl of cereal that took entirely too long to finish. Running back upstairs, she checked on Mom and Maxie to make sure they were getting dressed.

Lesson number one learned about her big brother: not a morning person. It had taken a good five or six trips to knock on his bedroom door before he finally whipped it open, glaring at her. He didn't have to be such a grump about it; they had a full itinerary and they needed to get an early start to fit everything in!

Maybe he was a coffee person. Sarah made a mental note to have some made tomorrow morning before he got up. . .and to *not* laugh at him if he greeted her like he had this morning. That would be a challenge, though. How could anyone do anything *but* fall down laughing at that murderous glare topped with flaming bedhead?

Sarah successfully corralled everyone into the car by ten, just as she had hoped. After a slight detour to Keelie's house to drop Diva off, they headed toward Seattle. Keelie had begged to meet Max, but Sarah held her off, promising she'd introduce them when they returned to pick Diva up at the end of the day.

"So, can you tell me now where we're headed?" Maxie turned from the passenger seat with a raised eyebrow.

"I can tell you where we're starting." She paused for dramatic effect. "Pike Place Market! Hopefully it won't be too crowded since it's just Wednesday morning and not the weekend. Have you heard of it before?"

"I think so. Something about throwing fish?" Maxie began, but then he appeared distracted by what he was seeing out the window. "Wait. Where are we now?"

"Uh. . .I don't know. On the road to Seattle? Mom?"

"This is Bellevue," Mom explained. "We're headed over Lake Washington on the 520 bridge into the city. Lake Washington is what separates Seattle from Bellevue and Kirkland."

"Wow. . . This is a *lake*? I thought it was part of Puget Sound; I've never seen a lake this big before. What mountain is that?" he asked, pointing toward their left.

"Ooo. . .I know that one," Sarah piped up. "That's Mount Rainier. It's an active volcano. Did you know that?"

"No," Maxie breathed as he stared out the window. "I mean. . .I've heard of the mountain, but. . .man, that thing is huge!"

"I know, right? Today we can see the whole thing, too. Lots of times the clouds hide the snow and ice toward the top."

"We have mountains back home—volcanos, even. Actually, we even have the tallest mountain in the world—Mauna Kea on the Big Island. But that's an inactive volcano and it looks nothing like this one because it's mostly under water. This thing is *massive*. It makes the peaks of O'ahu look like ant hills!"

Sarah had always enjoyed her view of the Olympic and Cascade mountain ranges that surrounded her home—especially the big peaks, like Rainier and Baker, but it seemed extra spectacular when enjoying it with Maxie for the first time. She smiled, thinking about all the other things they'd be seeing and doing for the first time together throughout the summer.

After surviving the daunting challenge of finding a place to park, they spent the remainder of the morning perusing the market. They started at the original Starbucks store—that had been Mom's choice. Then, after throwing a few coins in Rachel the Piggy Bank, they stopped by Daily Dozen Doughnuts for a bag of cinnamon-and-sugar-covered mini doughnuts to share. Next, they visited the fish market, where Maxie was entirely too interested in watching guys throw smelly, slimy dead animals around. Sarah didn't get the appeal. She imagined if they could, the fish would be thinking, *"Seriously? This is how you get your kicks?"* with a sigh and a roll of their dead little eyes as they flew through the air.

Sarah could stand it no longer, so she casually mentioned they weren't that far from the Gum Wall. That was a pretty disgusting sight, too—but less stinky—so she hoped to lure Maxie from the fish. Bingo. Not only was he satisfyingly stunned by the colorful display of discarded previously chewed treats all around him, but Mom happened to have some gum in her purse, so they added their own contributions to the spectacle as they contemplated different ways people had gotten their gum to stick up on the ceiling.

As they made their way through the rest of the market, Sarah reveled in the familiar assault on her senses—the smells of fresh fruits and veggies, roasted nuts, flowers and herbs; the sight of amazing artwork, crafts, and jewelry that she never had quite enough time to fully appreciate; the sounds of the bustling, growing crowd; and the amazing tastes of samples and snacks that just couldn't be passed up. It felt like just minutes had passed when Sarah realized it was already one o'clock. They needed to make their way back to Matt's In The Market for lunch.

The meal ended up being another potential disaster avoided. Sarah and Mom had made the reservations long before Maxie got into town, but they didn't know what kinds of food he liked. Luckily, he was happy with what he ordered. Better yet, he agreed with her that the Candy Bar Square they both ordered for dessert was *to die for*. Clearly, the boy had good taste. *Of course, he does*, Sarah thought with a shake of her head and a smile, *he's my brother*!

"So, what now?" Maxie asked as they made their way back out to the sunny street with freshly filled bellies.

"Now we catch the monorail so we can go tooooo. . .drumroll, please. . . The Space Needle!" she exclaimed with arms stretched wide. "No trip to Seattle is complete without an elevator ride to the tippy top of the Needle so we can check out all the sights. It'll be extra exciting, too, because they recently renovated it, so now there's an all-glass floor. Then up a little farther you can go outside on a landing, so there's no glass or anything between you and the view!"

Sarah glanced over at Maxie to catch his reaction, but instead of the eager enthusiasm she expected, she caught a brief expression of panic in his otherwise blank countenance that looked like he was carefully holding in place to hide his true feelings on her announcement.

Sarah had never considered Maxie might not enjoy the Space Needle. She loved the beautiful, expansive view from the top, but. . .what if Maxie was afraid of heights? Sarah couldn't relate to that fear, but she was deathly afraid of snakes. What if someone had come to her and said, "Surprise! We're going to visit the reptile section at the zoo and the zookeeper has agreed to take a boa constrictor out of the cage for us to hold and feed!"?

Her stomach revolted at the very idea. Oh, this wouldn't do at *all!* Today was supposed to be about Maxie feeling comfortable and loved and appreciated. She couldn't have him feeling fearful! But he was a 16-year-old boy. If she asked him outright if he was afraid of heights, he'd probably deny it, even if it was true. Had she imagined his response to her Space Needle announcement? No, his eyes had gone saucer-wide and his skin had definitely gotten pale (or, as pale as his beautiful, golden skin could get, anyway). Sarah nervously chewed on her thumbnail in thought as they boarded the monorail. She could ask Mom what to do, but she didn't want Maxie to think they were whispering about him—which is exactly what they'd be doing. How could she see if he was happy with the plan without embarrassing him?

As they exited the monorail, inspiration struck. "Wait!" she yelled, stopping short and throwing her arms out wide. Mom and Maxie stopped and turned to her with questioning looks. "Um. I forgot that the Space Needle is right next to MoPOP! Maxie, do you know what MoPOP is?"

At the shake of his head in the negative, she continued. "MoPOP stands for Museum of Pop Culture. It's all about music, science fiction and. . .well. . .pop culture. You know, I saw a few clouds when we were on the monorail. . ." Mom and Maxie both looked up at the pristine blue sky and looked back at Sarah with scrunched brows and narrowed eyes of confusion. "And I was just thinking," she quickly continued, hoping they wouldn't call her on the obvious fib, "You know what? We have *all summer* to check out the Space Needle. The best thing to see up there is Rainier, and we already saw that today, anyway. But I heard there's some really cool exhibits at MoPOP right now. Maybe it would be more fun to go there, instead. I mean—we could still go up the

Space Needle if you want, buuuttt. . ." she trailed off carefully studying Maxie's response.

With no hesitation, Maxie said, "No, no. MoPOP sounds cool. We can go there. You know. . .if you want." He threw in a casual shoulder shrug, but it didn't hide the relief Sarah had noticed pass over his face at her suggestion.

"Great!" Sarah exclaimed as they changed their direction toward the museum. She breathed her own deep sigh of relief. She had just successfully avoided potential catastrophe number three. Was she good, or *what*?!

The rest of the day passed without a hitch. Sarah was pleased to learn that her brother appeared to have as much geek in him as she had. They both tended to gravitate toward exhibits about fantasy, science fiction, myth, and magic. As fun as all that was, what had her leaving the museum with super sore abs was all the laughs they shared in the sound lab, experimenting with instruments and recording equipment. She was so in love with having someone to share all the fun and memories with!

They had a bit of a reprieve from all the activity when they went out for a great dinner, but they finished off their trip to the city with a Sounders game. Maxie was skeptical on the way into the stadium, declaring himself "more of a football guy."

Sarah laughed as he begrudgingly admitted on their way back over Lake Washington that watching a pro soccer game was pretty awesome, after all, and that he might be a new fan of the sport. She wasn't laughing at what he said, but at the whispery, growly hoarse voice he said it in after all his screaming and cheering at the game. He couldn't hear her laugh, though, because her own voice was too hoarse to make a sound.

They pulled into Keelie's driveway just after the sun had gone down, at about ten. It had been a long day, but a completely successful one, as far as Sarah was concerned. Keelie and Diva bounded out the front door of the house together as soon as the car had come to a stop. Keelie was just looking for an excuse to see Maxie; otherwise, she would have waited inside like any other time she had puppysat Diva.

Sarah made the introductions with a smile, more than happy to show off the best brother a girl could have to her best bud ever.

Maxie nodded and smiled politely, and Keelie awkwardly said hi with what Sarah would definitely consider a star-struck smile.

Keelie's older sister, Emmie, came out ranting, "Keelie, where did you put my phone charger?! I thought I told you to put it back on my desk when—" She stopped abruptly when she realized the size of her audience. "Oh. Hi, Sarah. I didn't realize you guys were back from Seattle."

"Yep!" Sarah confirmed. She was about to make another round of introductions, but she was interrupted.

"Hi," Maxie greeted Emmie—and suddenly his scratchy, gravelly voice sounded deeper, smokier and. . .sultry? "I'm Max. It's nice to meet you."

Sarah turned in time to catch the half smirk and head nod Maxie shot toward Emmie. It took every bit of self-control to keep from doubling over in laughter. She thought of the show *Friends* on Netflix and Joey's standard pick-up line, "How *you* doin'?"

Emmie offered a polite hello, apparently immune to the Maxie Flirt Smirk. Interesting. Sarah shot a glance over to Keelie, wondering if Maxie's apparent interest in Emmie would set off some sort of love-triangle battle. Kee appeared to notice the smoldering looks Maxie was sending Emmie's way, but she had either gotten over any mini-crush she had for her brother, or she was silently plotting Emmie's demise. Sarah made a mental note to keep a close eye on any relationship-type developments.

Within minutes they had Diva buckled up and they were on their way home. Sarah couldn't think of a time when she had felt more satisfied. It had been a spectacular day.

CHAPTER III

Max

Max looked around in disbelief. He was sitting in the walkout basement living room—the "screen room," Sarah had called it—not to be confused with the *other* living rooms of the house, the "family room" or the "den." He had a customized Minecraft Xbox controller in hand, playing Assassin's Creed on a screen the size of the entire wall. His feet were propped on a coffee table between bowls of pretzels and mixed nuts and a bottle of Honest Tea Sarah had brought down from the kitchen.

Next to him on the sofa, on what could only be described as a pink leopard-print throne, sat Diva. Luckily the tutu and tiara ensemble had been replaced with a relatively "tame" rhinestone collar. At least she now better resembled a dog. . .somewhat. A container of dog biscuits sat beside Max's snacks. He had endured no less than a half hour of instruction about how to give Diva a biscuit, how often to give them to her, and which of Diva's behaviors were deemed "biscuit-worthy." He huffed a small laugh, rolled his eyes, and shook his head at the memory of Sarah's ridiculously detailed tutoring session on puppysitting before her friend's mom swung by to pick her up for gymnastics practice. David and Rebecca were at work, so Max and Diva were alone in the house. Now he wondered if Sarah should have spent a minute or two longer explaining what cues Diva used for communication, as she seemed to have misinterpreted Max's laugh and head shake as a request for a thorough nostril cleaning. She was like an anteater searching out termites. He laughed harder and dodged his head in all directions, attempting to escape her ministrations without having to pause his game. Every time he thought this trip couldn't get more bizarre, the ridiculous factor seemed to be ratcheted up another notch.

He was saved from any further tongue-attack on his face when Diva suddenly launched herself off the couch and ran upstairs to greet whomever had just arrived home.

A few minutes later, David made his way into the room. "Hey," he greeted, crossing over to the recliner beside Max.

"Hi," Max responded distractedly, trying for the umpteenth time to make it through the level he was on.

David appeared to respect Max's need for uninterrupted time, raising Max's respect for him considerably. He even offered a helpful "go deep on stealth in the skill tree." The advice paid off; Max leveled up after an entire afternoon of previously failed attempts.

Okay, this guy wasn't so bad, after all. He looked over at his father, who was sipping from his bottle of some fancy flavored water. Max smirked and nodded his thanks and approval. "Do you wanna play some Smash Brothers?" was Max's peace offering.

"Sure!" David hopped up to switch over to the Nintendo system and give Max a new controller.

They filled the next hour with epic battle, punctuated by exclamations of "Oh, *whatever*!", "*Dude!* Where did you even come from on that one?!", "You are *so* going down!" and "Ha! Take *that!*"

David glanced at his phone and dropped his head to his chest, muttering, "Oh crap."

"What's up?"

"Well. . ." He sighed, reclining back farther in his seat. "I got yelled at the other day." He rubbed the heel of his hands over his eyes. "Rebecca informed me my airport pick-up performance was completely lacking."

"What? What do you mean? How would she know?"

"Oh, she knows all, believe me. That's a whole other story, though. She said I didn't talk with you nearly enough—you know, open up to you, get to know you better, blah, blah, blah."

Max raised his eyebrows, thanking David for falling short on whatever communication had been expected by Rebecca. He remembered how he had celebrated the lack of conversation on that car ride. Aside from the horrid choice in music, he thought everything had gone about as well as it could.

Conflicted feelings continued to jab and pull him in different directions, though. Questions continued to swirl. This whole situation was so *not normal*. Should he focus on his curiosity? His fears? The anger he discovered the night he'd arrived? What was someone supposed to feel in this type of situation? The whole thing made Max feel like a freak and he'd much rather just not face any of it. Heart-to-hearts meant exploring all that nonsense, and that was the last thing he wanted to do.

"I came home a little early tonight," David continued, pulling Max from his thoughts, "planning to do what she asked, but. . .I'm not so good at all that talking stuff. That's why I married an attorney; *she* does all the talking. She's excellent at it! Now she's due home in five minutes and we haven't *connected* the way she wanted us to."

"Well, she won't hear any complaints from me. We're good."

"Yeah?"

"Sure. Just tell her you went with the lesser known but highly effective method of male bonding known as the 'Smash Smackdown Session'."

Sarah ran into the room in a pink and purple leotard, covered in sweat and chalk. She threw herself into David's arms for a hug, immediately launching into a play-by-play of her day. *Yep,* Max thought, *let Sarah do all that mushy touchy-feely stuff. I'm good. I can go back home to my life on O'ahu in a few days and this whole trip will just be a bizarre memory.*

Sarah

"So, does she do this all the time, then?"

Sarah turned her attention from the TV to Maxie. "Does who do what?"

"Your mom. She's shut up in her office—*again.*"

"Oh." She nodded her head in understanding, then shrugged. "I don't know—she works quite a bit, I guess. . .sometimes more than others."

"Would you say the time since I've been here is one of those times when she has worked more than others?"

"No. I wouldn't say that." Sarah shook her head. "I mean. . .she even took the whole day off yesterday to take us into Seattle."

"Yeah, but you can't exactly call that a day off. She was on her phone pretty much non-stop the entire time."

"Noooo." Sarah mocked playfully, assuming he was joking.

Maxie raised his eyebrows, as if surprised by her reaction. "Uh, yeah she was," he argued with an almost apologetic smile.

"Oh. . .huh. . .I guess I didn't notice." She tipped her head to the side and scrunched her eyebrows together in thought. She vaguely remembered her mom talking on her phone from time to time, but she hadn't thought anything of it. "What does *your* mom do for work?"

"She's a yoga instructor, and she teaches hula. She does some underwater photography, too, but mostly the hula and yoga."

"Wow, that sounds *so cool!*" Sarah said dreamily. "Do you have a job, too? Is that why you have a lifeguard certificate?"

"Yeah. I've done some lifeguarding, but mostly I teach surfing."

"Wow, so you're, like, really into the ocean and stuff, huh?"

"Of course! Nothing can top the ocean; it's the best place in the world. Especially at the backdoor of some rad barrels." Maxie smiled as if riding a wave right now. He paused for a moment, then his expression darkened. "Too bad the mainlanders are doing all they can to *ruin* it," he said with a frustrated sigh, head-shake, and an eye-roll.

"What do you mean?"

"All the pollution. People fly to the islands for their vacations, and they have no respect for the environment. It's not just on the islands, though; trash finds us all the way from here."

"From *here?!* How is that?"

"It's all the plastics—like what you have in your hand right now."

Sarah looked down at her bottle of Vitamin Water, then looked back up at Maxie in silent question.

"A bunch of plastics like that end up in the ocean and the currents carry them right to our islands. When I was little, I didn't know anything about the currents and what they could carry; all I thought about was the waves. Now, though. . .now I go out and see way too much from humans in the water—bottles, shoes, plastic bags, *cell phones!*"

Sarah raised her eyebrows in disbelief.

Maxie continued, "Just a few weeks ago I came across a really sick-looking green sea turtle. I saw him when I was out surfing, but by the time I was done he had washed up onto the beach. I called the NOAA hotline because you're not allowed to touch them, since they're still a protected species. They picked him up and took him to a wildlife veterinarian." Maxie paused and shook his head, his eyes growing glassy. "I checked back the next day and found out he didn't make it. He had apparently eaten a balloon. The stupid thing even had a purple ribbon still attached. It blocked his digestive system, so he wasn't able to digest his food. He died of starvation. *Starvation!* They said that type of thing is happening more and more these days. Pff," he blew out disgustedly, "I hope whatever that balloon was celebrating was worth it!" He turned his attention back to the TV.

Sarah was stunned. . .and glad that Maxie turned away before he could catch her crying. The poor turtle! She looked down guiltily at the bottle in her hands. "That's terrible!" she whispered as she wiped her tears away. "I hadn't really thought too much about it. I'm going to make sure we don't buy these bottled drinks anymore; I'm going to start using a reusable water bottle."

"A cup works pretty well, too," Maxie pointed out with a smirk. Sarah was thankful for his attempt to lighten the mood. She didn't want to be a blubbering, bawling mess in front of him. One more turtle story and that's exactly what she'd be.

"A what, now? A. . .coop? A cop?" Sarah purposely mispronounced the word, teasing back with a smile. "What is this newfangled device you speak of?" Sarah's expression flashed from amused to startled. "Oh, I almost forgot. Your first day of work is tomorrow. Are you excited?"

"I don't know," he said with an uninterested shrug. "I guess it'll be better than sitting around the house all day."

"I have practice in the morning, but I'm going to try to go to the pool after that. Daddy said he could pick me up from the gym on his lunch break and drop me off at the pool, as long as a friend goes with me and can take me home. Keelie's tramp and tumble practice ends a half hour after my gymnastics practice, and she said she's down for some pool time. We just need to make sure her mom or sister can pick us up. As a matter of fact, I'm gonna check if she texted me back yet. Then I think I'll head to bed. Good night!"

Sarah stopped by the kitchen on her way upstairs and put her empty drink bottle in the recycling bin. She didn't think she'd ever hold another piece of plastic without thinking of Maxie's tragic turtle tale.

CHAPTER IV

Max

"Hi, are you Maddox?" inquired the tall guy who looked to be a couple years older than Max.

"Yeah. You can call me Max."

"Cool. I'm Aaron. And you're here until four today, right?"

"That's what I was told."

"All right, then. We open in a half hour; I'll show you around. Did you bring your lifeguarding certificate?"

"Yeah, the woman in the front office made copies of that and my CPR card."

"Nice." Aaron nodded his approval as he motioned toward the boys' locker room to begin their tour. "The showers are to the right, bathroom to the left, and the doorway out to the pool is straight ahead here," he explained as he continued outside.

Aaron lifted his arms to point to opposite ends of the pool. "There's two lifeguard chairs, one over there by the kiddie part of the pool, the other over here by the diving boards."

They continued to walk. "Over here is the towel booth." Aaron turned to the right, toward what looked to be the girls' locker room and a large window with a closed wooden shutter. He grabbed a key out of his pocket and unlocked the padlock holding the window shutter closed.

"So, there's three lifeguards on duty at all times and we rotate every hour on the hour. When you're not in one of the chairs, you'll be sitting in here hand-ing out towels and throwing the wet ones in the dirty towel cart. It gives you a chance to cool off and let your guard down for a little while. That's pretty much everything. Any questions?"

"Nope." Max shook his head. "That all seems pretty straightforward."

"Good. We have a little time before the pool opens. Lets' jump in for a quick cool-down."

They hopped in the pool, and Aaron struck up con-versation. "I haven't seen you around; are you new in town?"

"Yeah. I'm just visiting, actually. I'm from Hawaii. Dav—uh, my father—got me this job for while I'm here."

"Oh, so your whole family's here visiting, then?"

"No, my father lives here. My family is back home on O'ahu."

"Wow! I'd love to live on O'ahu! How often do you visit here?"

"Uh, actually this is the first time I've been to Washington."

"So, your dad just moved here, then?" Aaron asked, sounding confused.

"No," Max answered, "I think he's lived here for a long time." *I guess I should probably know how long he's lived here*, Max mused. *That seems like information a son would know about his father.*

"How often does your dad fly to Hawaii to visit you?"

"Actually, I just met him the other day," Max said with a smirk, attempting a casual, nonchalant attitude, but feeling nothing but embarrassed and awkward. What kind of freak just met his father for the first time at sixteen years old?!

Aaron turned in the water to face Max. "Oh, so the scum abandoned you—walked out on your mom and away from the responsibility of parenting, huh?" He shook his head and lifted the left side of his upper lip in apparent disgust. "Sorry, dude; I know what you're going through. Parents can really suck!"

"Wait—you know what I'm going through? You met your father as a teen, too?"

"Ha! I wish. No, he's been around forever. I'd love to never have to put up with his rules, disapproval, and rants, but there's no escaping him; he's *everywhere*," Aaron spat.

Max wondered what Aaron meant by 'he's everywhere,' but he shrugged it off. The other lifeguard had arrived, so they hopped out of the pool to open the doors. He took the whistle Aaron handed him and headed to the chair by the diving board.

Max had a whole hour to let his conversation with Aaron simmer. It hadn't really ever occurred to him to be angry with David for not being in his life before now. Makuahine had never seemed at all angry about not having David in their lives. The couple of times his father had come up in conversation, she said, "It just wasn't meant to be. We're on different paths." That's the type of person Makuahine was, though; she lived in the moment, finding the good in any situation and celebrating it. Had David taken advantage of his mother's sweet, trusting, and carefree nature? Maybe he *should* be angry with David; if not for his abandonment of him, for his mistreatment of Makuahine.

After a few hours, Sarah and her friend arrived at the pool. Sarah ran up to Max, acting like the overexcited, hyperactive puppy she tended to resemble. She introduced him to a number of people. As annoying as she was at times, Max had to admit it felt pretty good when she beamed up at him with pride as she gushed to whomever would listen about how she had the best big brother in the world.

*   *   *

"So, who was that little blond kid who kept bugging you all afternoon?" Aaron asked as they cleaned up around the pool at the end of the day.

"Hm? Oh, that was just Sarah. She's my sister."

"Wait, your dad had another kid after he took off on you?!"

"Uhhh. . .yeah. He married Sarah's mother, Rebecca, and then they had her." He shrugged.

"Ugh, half-sisters are the *worst!*" Aaron exclaimed. "They're all up in your business, never minding their own. Always causing trouble. . ." he trailed off, shaking his head with a disgusted sneer on his face, like he had some seriously unpleasant sister-related memories running through his head.

"Sarah's not all that bad. I mean, she's a spaz and all, which is annoying—especially the obnoxious way she wakes me up in the morning." Max paused a moment, considering his feelings about Sarah. "Of course, she's the one who apparently pushed for me to come here for this visit in the first place, so she definitely has that strike against her. You could be right; if she had just minded her own business, I'd probably be riding some sweet waves right now."

"Wait, *she's* the reason you're here?! Okay. . .I get it now."

"Get what?"

"Deadbeat Dad skips out on you and your mother without giving either of you a second thought—*until* his little precious princess expresses an interest in you. Then he's *all about* delivering her latest *toy* for her to play with. The spoiled little brat has probably gotten anything her heart desires her whole life!"

Max didn't even know what to think about Aaron's take on the situation. "Eh, family; whatareyagonnado, am I right?" he asked, feeling thoroughly uncomfortable and ready to change the subject.

"Yeah," Aaron said with a little smirk. "Hey," he continued in a much lighter tone as they walked through the locker room, shutting off the lights, "a bunch of us are headed to Totem Beach Park tomorrow night. You wanna come with us? It's not the white sandy beaches of O'ahu; it's not even the ocean, just a local beach here on Lake Washington, but it's usually a good time."

"Yeah, sure; sounds fun," Max agreed as they left the building, preparing to head their separate ways.

"Later, dude." Aaron offered a mock salute as he headed to the left, while Max turned toward the right.

"Later," he called over his shoulder. Max walked back to David's house, his mind spinning with new questions. Could David be the total Neanderthal Aaron had described? David hadn't made any attempt to explain why he had been absent from Max's life for so long. Could it be because David had no excuse to offer? And what about Aaron's take on Sarah? She was a nice enough kid, but was she just a spoiled brat? When she and her dog wore their matching tutus and tiaras, she certainly *looked* the part. Was Max truly nothing but a toy David had provided for his insistent princess—much like Makuahine had been for David years ago?—a toy just to be used up and thrown away?

A white-hot flash of rage exploded through Max at the thought. It was a completely unfamiliar and uncomfortable sensation, and just the fact that he was experiencing it made him resent David all the more. *What a fool I've been, not even seeing what was really happening right in front of my face,* Max thought in utter disgust as he walked through the front door of the house. *At least I have Aaron, now, to get me through the rest of this miserable trip.*

Fortunately, nobody else was home yet. Max didn't think he could face his father and remain civil. He threw together a quick sandwich and headed to his room, where he shut himself behind his door for the rest of the night.

*   *   *

"Hey!" Aaron nudged Max's shoulder as they passed one another during their rotation the next day. "See that kid over there in the green swim trunks?"

"Yeah."

"Keep an eye on him. He's been dunking that group of little kids over there all day."

"Oh. I didn't catch any of that from over on the other side of the pool," Max admitted as he took another look.

"Yeah. Don't take any of his crap, either. He always tries to pull the *Oh, poor innocent me* act, but he's total trouble more often than he's not. Don't hesitate to kick his butt out of the pool if you catch him trying to pull anything else."

"Thanks for the head's up, man."

Max settled into his chair overlooking dozens of swimming, splashing, and screeching kids. Not only was it a Saturday, but it was a particularly hot day, so the pool was at maximum capacity. That left absolutely no room for horseplay. He watched the crowd carefully, wanting to nip bad behavior in the bud before things got out of hand.

That was easier said than done. A kid cheating at Marco Polo freaked out when the rest of the players ganged up on him. A couple of teens were yelling and screaming at each other. Everyone at the pool soon knew every nauseating detail of their lovers' spat. As if that weren't bad enough, they later had a kiss-and-makeup session in the deep end of the pool that appeared suspiciously R-rated. And the only thing worse than having to say, "Diving is only allowed off the diving boards!", "No hanging on the ropes!", and "No running! Walk! . . . Walk!" thousands of times was having to follow them up with, "I *just* told you that five minutes ago!"

Max thought he was going to go deaf if he had to blow his whistle one more time. Then. . .he had to blow his whistle one more time. It was close to closing time, but Green Trunks apparently couldn't help himself from bullying some kid. It looked like he was trying to stomp the poor boy down to the bottom of the pool. Max didn't waste any time. He blasted his whistle long and hard, pointing directly at Green Trunks when all eyes turned to see who was in trouble. "You! Outta the pool, buddy! You're done for the day!"

"*What?!*" the kid cried, indignant. "What'd I do?! I didn't do nothin'!"

"I don't want to hear it, buddy. You could have drowned that kid!"

"What do you mean?!" He protested in a high screechy voice as Max took him by the arm, leading him to the locker room. "We were just kiddin' around! He just did the same thing to me a minute ago! He wanted to see if I could hold him up on my shoulders and then we wanted to see if he could hold me up on his!"

"Whatever, dude. You've been dunking kids all day, and you can't be doing that. Someone will get hurt or even drown! You're done."

"You're crazy, man! I wasn't dunkin' kids!" Green Trunks continued to yell and scream as he slammed the locker door after grabbing his clothes. "This is B.S., and you're not gonna get away with it!"

Max shook his head with a heavy sigh as he made his way back out to the pool. Green Trunks had carried on like he lost out on the pool for the entire day, not just the last half hour. He should have considered himself lucky.

Fortunately, the last thirty minutes of work were uneventful. Then they were finally able to kick *everyone* out of the pool. "Hey, where's the beach you were talking about last night?" Max asked Aaron as they cleaned up the locker room. "And what time is everyone meeting up?"

"I have my truck, so we can just leave from here if you want. There's a burger place near the beach, so we can grab a bite when we get there."

"Cool! Sounds good to me!"

Finishing up the last of their work, they headed out to the lone vehicle still parked in the lot—a Hummer. *You've gotta be kidding me,* Max thought with a shake of his head as he heaved himself up into the passenger seat. *Are there any vehicles in this town that* aren't *gas-guzzling giants?! And how can Aaron even afford this monstrosity? He's a lifeguard! Lifeguard wages don't buy Hummers!*

After binging out on burgers, fries, and chocolate shakes, Aaron and Max made the short walk to the beach. Aaron had been right with his description of the beach—it was certainly a lot different from his beaches back home on O'hau. There was no hypnotic ebb and flow of the ocean waves in his ears, no sea-salt spray tickling his nose. The sand between his toes was just enough to make him a little homesick, but the rest of the experience was all new and unfamiliar to him.

A long wooden dock jetted out into the water to the left. Seattle's skyline offered a sweet view across the wide expanse of water, slightly to the right, and the daunting, yet majestic view of Mount Rainier arose in the distance straight ahead. The beach was not particularly big, but there was a scenic trail leading along the water's edge beyond the dock that Aaron said led through some marshlands and on into the forest.

Within a few minutes of their arrival, guys who appeared to recognize Aaron made their way onto the beach. Max didn't know most of them, but he recognized a few from the pool. Kiss-and-make-up guy was among them. Max wondered if he was on the outs with his girlfriend again or if she would show up at some point and they'd be all over each other again. About a dozen guys in all took a dip to cool off, then made their way to the athletic field across the street. One of the guys had a football, so they started a game.

Max was still emotionally keyed up after his chat about family with Aaron the day before. He decided getting a little winded and blowing off some steam on the field was probably best before he talked to David or Sarah again.

The physical exertion felt good after a full day of sitting on his butt by the pool. He was having fun, but as the game progressed, a group of three guys on the opposing team were irritating him as they got increasingly rowdy. Their laughs were just a little too loud, their hits just a little too hard, and their trash talk had turned into taunts and insults.

"Just a wild guess," Aaron murmured as they broke from a huddle, "but I don't think that's water in their water bottles."

Max glanced at the sidelines where the Three Musketeers, as he had started to think of them, made their way back to the center of the field after taking a "water break." He had to agree with Aaron's assessment. They were giggling. *Giggling!* Added to the fact that they were stumbling over their own feet, that made for rather conclusive evidence they were probably pretty wasted.

On the next play, the quarterback on Max's team handed the ball off to a skinny little eighth or ninth grader who easily wiggled past all three boozed-up blockheads and ran in for a touchdown. Suddenly the musketeers weren't finding any humor in the situation. They appeared to take a particular dislike to the touchdown dance Skinny Kid was performing.

"Oh, what? You think because you made one lucky play squeezing your skinny ass through us that now you're on your way to the NFL, there Sport?" the lead lughead taunted as they stalked toward him.

Max followed, anticipating trouble. He arrived at the endzone just as the ringleader shoved Skinny to the ground. Without thinking, Max plowed into the big oaf, growling, "Pick on someone your own size, moron!"

Slam! Max sucked in a wheezing breath, immediately regretting that decision when his mouth and nose filled with dirt and grass. He couldn't be sure, but it appeared he had been tackled from behind by the two other musketeers and they were now pig piling him. Grunting with effort, he scrambled his arms around in search of leverage to push himself free. In the struggle to turn himself over, his leg swung out and his knee made contact with something.

"You idiot! You just gave me a freakin' bloody nose!"

Oh. That's what he had hit. Max used the moment of chaos to his advantage, working himself out from under them and springing back to his feet. He considered patting himself on the back for successfully fighting off two guys singlehandedly—or, maybe more accurately, single-knee-edly—but he decided to remain modest about his triumph. After all, his adversaries were nothing more than a couple of sluggish, uncoordinated bumbling-drunk nincompoops. Their most potent weapons had been their dead weight and ridiculously bad breath that reeked of alcohol.

The rest of the players had arrived on the scene. Some seemed to be trying to help defuse the situation, others seemed all too happy to jump into the fray. Max searched for Skinny to ensure the kid hadn't been pulled back into the brawl. Luckily, he had made it safely to the sidelines, well out of danger. The same couldn't be said for Aaron. Not only was he in the thick of the battle, but he seemed to be loving every minute of it. Max assumed that meant Aaron could handle himself, so he decided to just stay out of the way.

The commotion lasted a few minutes longer before the guys with calmer heads were able to neutralize the troublemakers. The three musketeers were hauled off to the car of the kid who was apparently acting as their designated driver. They were starting to look a bit green and Max was reasonably sure at least one would puke before they got home. By the worried expression the driver wore, he seemed to agree with Max's prediction.

Skinny headed home on his bike, and the rest of the crowd scattered to go their separate ways. "Whew! That was fun, huh?" Aaron asked as he and Max walked down the sidewalk toward the Hummer.

Max couldn't help but notice Aaron's excited tone, huge smile, exaggerated swagger, and the way he swiveled his head, as if looking for an excuse to clash with someone else. "I don't know if I'd say *fun*," he countered, "but it definitely got my adrenaline pumping!"

"Exactly! And you even got *two* chances at it today!"

Max shot Aaron a look of confusion.

"First you saved a swimmer from probably being drowned when you hauled that punk twerp out of the pool," Aaron explained, "and just now you rescued that little kid from being pummeled by a pack of drunk dimwits. There's no better way to work out your frustrations than by whoopin' some butt, and you had the perfect excuse to do just that *twice* today!" He paused as he pushed the button on the fob to unlock the doors on the Hummer. "I know you've been holding in some major aggravation and irritation over the whole situation with your good-for-nothing father," he continued. "You *have* to admit it feels danged good to pound a little of that annoyance out on some losers with the best excuse ever—playing the hero."

Max mulled over what Aaron had said as he hopped up into the passenger seat. He *was* feeling more relaxed than he had been the previous evening, and that *did* feel good. Was it the exercise and fresh air? The friendly football game—before it got less than friendly? Or *was* it the excitement and sense of power he felt, having fought off three dudes? Maybe Aaron was right. If so, he could certainly get used to it.

CHAPTER V

Sarah

"I don't know, Kee; I just thought it would be different, I guess." Sarah sighed as she relaxed back against the headboard of her bed and extended her left arm out to judge her paint job on her nails.

"He hasn't even been here a full week, though," Keelie countered from the beanbag chair, as she absently scrolled her Instagram feed. "You can't expect a ready-made sibling relationship the minute he walks through the door. You need to give it some time. Plus, you need to remember you can't get your hopes up too high. As shocking as it may sound, *occasionally* siblings don't get along."

"I know, but...I was just so hopeful Maxie and I would grow close," Sarah grumbled, shaking her hand and blowing on her nails, trying to speed along the drying process. "Last night I didn't even see him at all after I got home from practice. He was in his room and refused to come out!"

"Wait. A teenaged boy was locked away in his room? Quick! Call the press; that *never* happens!"

"I know, right? Someone needs to tell him that that's just not *done!*" Sarah smirked, playing along despite having conceded Keelie's sarcastic point.

"We'd better get downstairs and start watching for Emmie. She said if she had to text me that she's here to pick me up again, it would be the last ride she'd ever give me." Keelie rolled her eyes as she stood up. "I mean, it only happened *once* when we lost track of time, playing Sims! She'd probably disown me if she had to—*gasp!*—get *out* of the car and knock on the door. Honestly, I don't know why you'd ever be so excited to get an older sibling. They're such a pain in the butt!"

The girls made their way out to the front yard to wait for Emmie. A huge black vehicle pulled up to the curb in front of the house, and Maxie jumped out of the passenger seat.

"Maxie!" Sarah yelled with unsuppressed glee as she jumped up off the ground and ran toward him. When he hadn't come home after the pool closed, she feared she wouldn't see him all night again. She pulled herself up just shy of jumping into his arms for a huge bear hug. She didn't want to scare him away. The last time she had offered an exuberant hug he seemed to be a little thrown off. Maybe he wasn't a hugger. . .yet.

"Who was that?" she asked, as the car Maxie had ridden up in drove away.

"Just a guy from work—Aaron. Why?"

"Just curious. I don't think I've seen that car around the neighborhood before."

"Probably gets lost among the masses of overpriced monstrosities."

Sarah was about to ask him what he meant by that when Emmie's familiar purple VW Bug pulled up. She turned back to where her friend had been sitting on the grass. Staring dreamily at Maxie, Keelie hadn't noticed her sister's arrival. The words "Emmie's here" were on Sarah's tongue, ready for release, but Maxie's voice halted them.

"Hey," he said, standing next to the driver's side door of the Bug. "You're Emmie, right?"

"Yeah," she confirmed with a smile. "And you're Max, yeah?"

Maxie nodded with a smirk. "What are you up to tonight?" he boldly asked.

"Just picking my little sister up to go home for family movie night."

"Right on." Maxie nodded, as if approving.

Emmie shocked Sarah by continuing. "But tomorrow a bunch of us are headed to the beach to hang. Wanna come along? We're all meeting up around seven."

"Totem Beach?"

"Yeah! You know it?"

"I'm familiar." Maxie turned his attention to Sarah. "We don't have anything going on tomorrow night, do we?"

"Um, Daddy said he was going to take us all to—" Sarah stopped herself short. Daddy had said he'd take them for a hike around Snoqualmie Falls, but with Maxie's aversion to heights, hanging out to gawk at a 250-plus-foot waterfall would probably not go over very well. "...Um..." she stalled while she scrambled to come up with an alternate plan. "I think he said he was going to take us all to the Museum of Flight...or something..."

"That wouldn't keep us out until after seven, though, right?"

"No. We should definitely be back by then," Sarah assured him.

"Awesome. Looks like I'll be seeing you at the beach." Maxie flashed Emmie a big smile.

Keelie was in the car and buckled up, so Emmie called out, "Great! See you at seven, then!" and drove off.

Maxie stood on the side of the street and watched as the purple Bug made its way around the cul-de-sac and back out toward the main road. He was rewarded with a smile and wave from Emmie. *Huh*, Sarah thought. *Maybe Emmie wasn't so immune to Maxie's Flirt Smirk the other night, after all! Interesting.*

Mom and Dad were out on a date night and Maxie had already eaten, but he said he wouldn't be opposed to eating more if there was more to eat, so Sarah made up a box of mac 'n' cheese and a frozen pizza for them to share. Inspired by Keelie's family movie night, she asked Maxie to pick out a movie while she finished the cooking.

Then Sarah enjoyed an awesome evening that matched her dreams almost perfectly. Maxie had chosen one of the *Guardians of the Galaxy* flicks, and instead of munching on popcorn together as she had pictured so many times over the years, it was pizza and pasta they chowed down on while laughing and cheering through the movie together.

This.

This is what she had been wanting for *so long*, and she reveled in every moment of it.

*   *   *

"Daddy, how much longer before we get home?" Sarah asked as they made their way back from the museum.

"About fifteen minutes."

"Would you mind dropping Maxie and me off at Totem Beach? A bunch of my friends want to hang out for a little while. They said they would be there at seven, and it's already 6:15."

"*Who* all will be there? And what are you going to do at the beach? You don't even have bathing suits or towels."

"It's mainly kids from the gym who will be there; we've been group texting about it. As for being prepared, I have that covered. This morning I threw a bag in the trunk with my suit and a few towels. As for Maxie. . ." Sarah looked over at her brother to appraise his attire. Yep. He had on another pair of board shorts. "I don't think he owns anything *but* swim trunks. That's what those are, right?"

Maxie nodded.

"How and what time do you plan on getting home?" Dad interrogated further.

"Emmie said she'd drive us home. I don't know what time, exactly. Maybe by. . .ten?" Sarah offered, fingers crossed that Dad would go for it.

"I don't think so. I'll drop you off there, but you need to be home by nine. And call me if *anything* changes or doesn't go as planned, okay?"

"Okaaayyy." Sarah drew out the word. She had hoped that having Maxie with her would translate into a later curfew, but she accepted Dad's terms.

"Max, will you please keep an eye out for Sarah, make sure she stays safe?" Dad asked.

"Sure," Max agreed.

Max

"Hey, dude. I didn't know you'd be here tonight," Max greeted Aaron.

"Eh, there was nothing going on at home, so I thought I'd see what action we might drum up here," Aaron responded as he took a look around the beach. "Your pops didn't just bring you here as a toy but as a baby-sitter, too, huh?" he added as he spotted Sarah in a huddled group of girls.

"No. Not really."

"Oh yeah? You're saying they haven't left her with you at all since you've been here?" Aaron countered skeptically.

"Well. . .a few times. It was no big deal, though. . ." Max trailed off, mentally counting the times he had been left alone at the house with Sarah. Would she have stayed home alone, otherwise? Would David have had to hire a sitter if he hadn't come to Washington? Was his father taking advantage of him?

Max shook off the questions, trying to focus on the situation at hand. "Anyway, Emmie invited me here. She's over there—the one in the pink top and blue shorts." He indicated who he was talking about with a subtle toss of his head in her direction. "I didn't know Sarah and Emmie's little sister would be coming, too, but. . .whatever."

"Oh, you thought this was gonna be more of a date, huh?" Aaron teased.

"Well. . ." He let the word drag out. "I wouldn't say that, but I certainly wouldn't mind getting to know her a little better. She's pretty cute."

"That she is," Aaron agreed with a slow, thoughtful nod as he looked over in Emmie's direction. "That she is," he repeated quietly, almost as if speaking to himself. He took another sweeping look around the beach. "Hey," he said with some urgency, "just a head's up; see that guy over there with the baseball cap on backwards?"

"In the red shirt? Yeah."

"Before you got here, he was really getting handsy and hassling those girls your sister and her friends are standing with over there. He just can't seem to take no for an answer. Keep an eye on him. I can't imagine how much trouble you'd get into if anything happened to that princess half-sister of yours."

Max sneered in disgust. He hated idiots like that who gave all guys a bad name. "Got it. Thanks, man."

Sarah

"Diva!" Sarah yelled as she squatted in the sand and opened her arms wide.

Diva ran across the beach with her leash trailing behind her. She jumped up on her hind legs and gave kisses of greeting with enough enthusiasm and excitement to knock Sarah onto her back. Sarah giggled with delight, attempting to keep her mouth closed to avoid the dog's expert probing tongue. She loved these moments; Diva always made her feel so loved and appreciated.

Eventually she cuddled her pup to her chest and got up to greet her friends. "Hey, everybody! Oh, and thank you so much for puppysitting today, Lexi!"

"My total pleasure," Lexi gushed. "She is so fun! *Any time* you need someone to watch her, be sure to call me!"

"But only if I'm not available to do it!" Keelie threw in with a smile. "Actually, why don't you hand her over now. I'll watch her while you go to the bathroom and get your suit on."

As Sarah made her way back to the beach from the bathroom, she broke into a run and opened her arms wide again, this time to welcome a couple of late-comers walking over from the parking lot. "My! Ty! Ohmygod, it's so good to see you two. I was worried you weren't able to make it!" Mylee and Tyler were two of her gym mates on the Trampoline and Tumbling team with Keelie. "Come on! Everybody's over here! Oh, and I need to introduce you guys to my big brother, Maxie, too. You're gonna love him!"

Everyone took a dip to cool off, bickering good-naturedly over who's turn it was to get out of the water and sit with Diva. Then they all made their way over to a picnic table where a few of the girls had brought some snacks. Sarah looked for Maxie so she could invite him over to meet everyone, but it looked like he was playing soccer with some guys. She smiled, remembering the fun they had at the Sounders game.

Sarah was moseying through the group, chatting and laughing with everyone, when she noticed Keelie sitting quietly to the side. She made her way over and plopped down next to her best friend. "Wuzzup, girlfriend?"

"Nothing much," Keelie mumbled as she scratched Diva's belly.

Sarah knew that tone. *Nothing much* was definitely *something*. She scanned the park, wondering if she could spot the cause of Keelie's blue mood. "Oh," she breathed out, sure she had figured it out. "Is it Emmie? Emmie and Maxie?"

Keelie looked up in confusion, then followed Sarah's eyes over to the sports field. Emmie was talking with Maxie on the sidelines, and judging from the smiles and laughs, it looked like she was really enjoying their chat. "No, it's not Emmie."

"But I thought you liked Maxie."

"Don't get me wrong; he's cute and all, and he seems really nice. He's just. . .fun to look at, know what I mean? There's someone else I've been thinking about. . .you know. . .fo' realz, but. . .it's not going to work out."

"You don't know that! You're awesome! Anyone would totally be lucky to go out with you! Who is it? We'll see if we can make this happen."

"No. I *know* it won't work. See, I. . .I've really been enjoying hanging out with Ty lately. He goes to a different school, so I didn't see him much until this summer, when there's more time to hang out."

"Ty?! He's so sweet! What's the problem? I'm sure he'd love to go out with you!"

"Eh. He *might have*, but. . .I just found out he and My are officially dating now."

"Shut. Up! Are you serious?! Mylee and Tyler? Oh," Sarah consoled as she pulled Keelie into a side hug. "I'm so sorry!"

"Yeah, well. . .it's okay. I just needed a minute, ya know?"

"Sure. Sure. I'll stay here with you. Diva was getting a little agitated with all the activity over there in the big group, anyway."

"Thanks, Sar-Bear." Keelie rested her head on Sarah's shoulder.

Sarah sat in quiet solidarity with her friend for a few minutes, then tried to lighten her mood with a little humor. "So, like. . .will their official couple name be MyTy?" She smirked. "Will they go around everywhere with a little paper umbrella? You know, like a Mai Tai, the drink? Get it?" She giggled.

Keelie bumped her in the shoulder playfully, smiling and rolling her eyes. "Yes, I get it!" She spoke the words up toward the sky, as if totally exasperated. She looked back down at her friend. "And I love you, Sarah, but don't quit your day job. Leave the comedy to the professionals."

Sarah laughed, but her mirth was suddenly interrupted by a massive commotion over by the picnic table. People were yelling and had formed a circle. Sarah and Keelie stood up to get a better view. It appeared to be a fight. *Who would be fighting?!* Sarah wondered in alarm.

Just then she saw it. Flames. There was no mistaking Maxie's unique hair. Her brother was in a fistfight with someone! Panicked, she ran over to the ring of spectators, unable to sit idly by, but with no idea what she might possibly do to help. By the time she got there, though, the scuffle had been broken up, the fighters each pushed off in a different direction.

"Maxie!" she yelled as she wormed her way into the group pushing her brother away from the scene of the battle. "Maxie, what happened?!"

"Nothing, Sarah; don't worry about it," came his surly response.

"Come on," Emmie said, "Let's pack up. It's probably about time we head out anyway."

As Sarah grabbed her towel from the beach, she couldn't help but notice the breathtaking magnificence of a brilliant sunset. The water sparkled with flecks of gold. A few clouds along the horizon glowed, as if on fire. The rest of the sky soothed with a calming array of pastels. She had trouble reconciling the peaceful splendor she saw before her and the chaos and confusion she was about to walk back toward.

The hum of the car motor seemed unreasonably loud in the absence of any music or chitchat on the way home. Sarah wanted to open all the windows and blow out the awkward silence that hung over everyone. She was relieved when it was time to wish the girls a good night and shut the car door. Once inside the house, Maxie went straight up to his room without a word.

Sarah found Dad in the screen room. He seemed pretty into whatever sci-fi action flick he was watching, so she just gave him a kiss and hug and let him be. She found Mom in her bed, surrounded by paperwork.

"How was the beach, sweetie?" Mom greeted with a smile as she pushed her glasses up on top of her head.

"It was good." Sarah hoped she'd be able to get through the conversation without having to go into detail about all that had happened. She didn't want to betray Maxie by tattling on him. "A lot of the kids were there from gym, so. . .it was fun!" She punctuated the final words with a smile and head nod that she hoped said, *Okay? And that's all there is to say about that, soooo. . .I guess we're done here!*

"Oh good! It's always so nice have a chance to see your teammates outside of the gym." Mom smiled briefly, then transitioned to her *Mom Voice.* "Make sure you hang your wet suit and any wet towels up to dry. Do *not* leave them in your bag to get all moldy." In case the tone wasn't enough, she tucked her chin down and raised her eyebrows to include the *Mom Look*.

"Yep. I'm on my way to do that right now!" Sarah kissed and hugged Mom good night and ran out of the room. She shook her head in disbelief that she had just been *saved* from possibly having to spill on the beach details by a *Nag Attack*. Who would have guessed she'd ever feel thankful for being pestered by her mom?!

On the way to her room, Sarah stopped at Maxie's door, hand raised, ready to knock. *Is he okay? What happened? Will being in a fight make him want to go back to Hawaii? Is this something he's done often?* She guessed, though, that Maxie wouldn't welcome any of those questions. Maybe he'd be more in the mood to talk about it in the morning after a good night's sleep. She backed away from the door and quietly padded to her room, itching to be whisked away to distant lands and times by her *Big Book of Greek Mythology*. Reading about the woes of the gods always seemed to help put her petty problems in perspective.

The next morning Sarah woke early, determined to make it a great day for everyone in the family. It was Monday, so Mom and Dad had work, Maxie would be going to the pool early for a training session, and she needed to get Diva down the street for her puppy playdate with Lucky.

She brewed the coffee she knew the rest of her family would appreciate and started preparing French toast for anyone interested in joining her for breakfast. As she whipped the eggs and milk, she heard Dad behind her, retrieving something out of the cabinet. She began to turn and wish him a good morning, but Maxie walked into the room and caught her attention. His colorful bangs were hanging unusually low over his right eye, but from her angle she couldn't help but notice a big black and purple ring. She gasped, and without thinking, blurted out, "Oh my god! Maxie, that guy gave you a black eye!"

Immediately realizing her mistake, she threw her hand over her mouth, as if trying to stuff the wayward words back in.

Maxie glared at her and Dad spun around toward them, erupting, "*What?!*" in a tone she couldn't remember ever hearing from him before.

"You got into a *fight?!*" Dad demanded, red-faced. "In front of your *sister*, no less?!" he added, incredulously, throwing his hands onto his hips.

"No. It's not like that—" Maxie began to explain or maybe defend himself.

"I don't know what you do back in Hawaii," Dad interrupted, "but we do *not* condone physical violence in this house! Do you understand me?!" He didn't wait for a response. "I will *not* have Sarah exposed to such behavior!"

A flash of hurt crossed Maxie's face. Then he erupted, too. "*Fine!* You won't have to worry about me corrupting your precious princess ever again! I'm outta here! I never even wanted to come here in the first place!" He left those words hanging in the air as he spun on his heel and retreated up the stairs to his room, slamming his door behind him.

"Ugh. . ." Dad groaned, rubbing the heels of his hands over his eyes. "That could have gone better." He sighed heavily, shaking his head. "So, tell me about this fight your brother was in last night."

"I don't know. I mean. . .I don't think it was anything, really." Sarah stumbled over her explanation. Her brain raced, trying to come up with a way to minimize the situation to the point where Dad would just drop it. "I mean. . .I looked toward a commotion, thought I saw a fight, but before I even realized what was going on, it was over." She threw in a shoulder shrug to emphasize the insignificant nature of the incident.

"Uh-huh."

Sarah squirmed under Dad's intense scrutiny. Finally, he released her from the vice-like grip of his stare-down when he turned back to the counter and popped a lid onto his travel mug. "Well," he said, sighing, "we'll revisit this conversation when I get home tonight. Unfortunately, I have a meeting I have to get to right now. Maybe it's for the best that we both have some time to cool down first, anyway. Love you, and have a good day, kiddo." Dad pulled Sarah into a quick hug, then headed into the garage and off to work.

Mom was just entering the kitchen as Dad left, taking some yogurt out of the refrigerator for breakfast. "Morning, sweetie! Did you sleep okay?"

"Uh. . .yeah, sure," Sarah answered distractedly, still freaked out over the yelling match she had just witnessed.

"I thought I heard something bang or slam when I was drying my hair. Did you drop something in here?" Mom looked around, as if searching for evidence of a dropped plate or coffee mug.

"Uh, no. I didn't hear anything. That's strange. Maybe it was something outside?" Sarah kicked herself for not thinking more quickly on her feet. She could have said she had dropped a cast-iron skillet on the floor or something. She knew it wasn't right to lie to her mother, but she didn't want to explain why Maxie slammed his bedroom door.

"Oh. Huh. Maybe." Mom shook her head, as if physically shaking off her curiosity. "Anyway, you'll be going to the Thompsons' house today with Diva, right?"

"Yes," Sarah answered enthusiastically, relieved that Mom had dropped the subject of loud, disturbing noises. "I'm just going to shower, get dressed, and I'll head over later this morning."

"Okay. Max is upstairs? And he'll be here until after you've left?" Mom quizzed as she prepared her coffee in the travel mug Sarah had gotten her for her birthday.

"Yeah."

"Good. But I still want you to text me when you leave here and when you get to the Thompsons'."

"Mom, they live *two doors down!*"

"So, I still worry about my baby girl. Sue me!" Mom smiled over her shoulder.

Sarah rolled her eyes. "I'm not a *baby* anymore. And isn't suing you what everyone *else* does?"

Mom chuckled. "They wouldn't dare. I'd beat their butts out of the courtroom every time. And don't change the subject! You are going to text me when you leave here, when you get there, and when you get back home, right?" She raised her eyebrows and cocked her head to the side expectantly.

Sarah sighed. "Fine. I'll even throw in a text when I eat, when I pee, and any time I scratch my left ear."

"Oh, good. Hit me up with one every time your right eyebrow twitches, too," Mom played along. "And you know I always appreciate updates on the status of your spleen. Keep me posted!" She paused and hugged Sarah. "Gotta run; I have a deposition first thing this morning. Bye. Love you. I won't be home from work when you get back, but hopefully I won't be too late tonight."

"Love you, too."

When Mom exited the kitchen, the house felt too quiet. Sarah felt small, anxious, unsettled, and uncomfortably isolated. She had spent plenty of time alone in her house before, but never with family tension swirling around her, thick and foreboding.

Disappointed by losing this chance to share time with her family, she put away the egg-and-milk mixture for another time. She had lost her appetite.

She considered trying to talk to Maxie as she made her way up the stairs, but something told her she wouldn't be welcome. She slumped as she reached the top step, deciding to quietly pass Maxie's room and just get ready for Diva's playdate, as planned. Hopefully Dad was right. Hopefully the day would offer clarity and perspective, so they could all go back to the warm, loving family they had started to become.

Right now, Sarah's plan to bring her family together felt like it had completely gone off the rails.

CHAPTER VI

Max

"**D**uuuudde! Look at you with your savage shiner!" Aaron greeted with a huge smile and nod of approval when Max arrived at the pool. "It's a good look. It says, *Don't give me any crap* and *You should see the other guy*. You're totally rockin' it, bro!"

"Funny. According to David it says, *I'm a juvenile delinquent, I'm a bad influence* and *I'm not worthy to be a member of this household*. I'm thinking it means I don't belong here. This place sucks and I'm ready to go home."

"Ah, don't say that, man!" Aaron slashed his arm in front of him, as if batting away Max's idea of leaving. "The parental unit will chill; just give it a minute. We're having too much fun to give up on the summer now!"

"Ha! Yeah. *Fun.* I've been in two fights since I got here less than a week ago. I had never been in a *single* fight before that in my entire life!"

"That just means you're growing up. A man has to fight for the things he stands for." Aaron paused, taking in Max's disbelieving scowl. "You know, I hung around after the dust settled last night and gathered some intel. That kid you fought? 'Mr. Handsy?' His name is Towa. First of all, he definitely didn't fare as well as you. He has double shiners and a busted lip. He was pissed for being called out on being the slime-bag he is. He found out who you are and said he'll be here tomorrow when the pool closes to 'give you what you have coming.' Can you believe that?! Not only does he think it's cool to hit on girls and put his hands all over them whether they like it or not, but he thinks it's all good to ambush you after work in some pathetic attempt to prove his manliness."

"*What*?! What is *wrong* with people here?!" Max sighed heavily, shaking his head. He had never been a fan of fighting before, but it seemed some pinheads needed a physical reminder that they should act more like gentlemen. Picturing Sarah, Emmie, and the rest of the girls, and thinking about what could have happened to any one of them if he hadn't put a stop to it, effectively quieted any inner voice that told Max fighting wasn't the answer. He'd show this Towa the error of his ways. He'd knock some sense into the doofus—*again*—to make his point clear. "Know what? I'll be ready for him. He'll regret not learning his lesson the first time around!"

Max spun back toward the doors to let the swimmers in. He glanced back to see that a huge grin had spread across Aaron's face.

Sarah

Sarah's head was spinning as she walked home from Diva's puppy playdate. She had been so distracted early in the morning that she hadn't checked her phone until she got to the Thompsons'. She had missed four calls and twenty-four messages. The calls were from Keelie and Sarah's teammate, Adele. The messages were from her entire team—she had been included in six group texts. Glancing through them, she discovered that the guy Maxie had fought the night before was Adele's older brother, Towa. There were all sorts of declarations that *no way* Towa deserved to be attacked that way, and that Maxie was a total brute and should have his butt kicked back to Hawaii. Then there were pages and pages of theories on what might have sparked the fistfight.

Mom hadn't allowed Sarah to use social-media sites yet, but she imagined there was a constant stream of chatter on SnapChat and Instagram on the matter, too. Some people had texted pics and videos of "The Big Event" they had posted online. What a nightmare!

Never, in all her dreams of life with an older brother, had Sarah imagined her friends turning against her because of him. How had she so misjudged Maxie? She couldn't reconcile the troublemaker everyone took him for and the sweet guy who told tales of attempted turtle rescues with tears in his eyes.

Walking in through the front door, she paused and listened for any sign someone was home. Noise was coming from downstairs in the screen room. She headed down and found Maxie playing Halo.

"Hey," she greeted quietly.

He shot her a quick glance, but continued to play. "Hey."

"Sooo. . .how was *your* day?" Sarah sat in the chair next to the couch where Maxie was sitting.

"Fine." Maxie continued to click furiously on the controller, apparently attacking some bad guy.

When he didn't politely return concern over the success of her day, Sarah continued with a less-than-subtle prompt. "My day kinda sucked."

"Oh yeah?" Maxie asked distractedly, sticking his tongue out of the side of his mouth, apparently attempting a complex maneuver.

"Yeah." Sarah was irritated by his complete lack of sympathy and annoying refusal to play along properly in the conversation. "Because last night *you* decided to attack some unsuspecting, innocent guy for no apparent reason *whatsoever*. Now *my* phone has been blowing up *all day* with everyone wanting to know what the heck Your. *Problem. Is*! I mean. . .seriously! This is *not* the way having you here was supposed to go!"

"*Really?*" Maxie exploded, tossing the controller to the side and shifting his attention to Sarah. "And how was it *supposed to go*?" He surrounded the last three words with air quotes. "Was I supposed to be a good little *toy* for you to play with all summer?"

"*No!* I—wait, *what?!* What are you even *talking about?!* I don't even. . . *What?!*"

"Did you think I wouldn't figure it out, *Princess*? David doesn't give a rip about me my *whole life*, but suddenly his little Queen of Quite-A-Lot decides she's bored and needs something new to play with. You bat your little eyes and snap your little fingers and he totally *jumps* to give you whatever the heck your heart desires—a new *toy* for the summer!"

Sarah's chest literally sunk back as if his words had physically slammed her in the ribs. "I don't even. . . How?. . .That's. . .that's really what you *think?!*" The words squeezed through her tightening throat, rough and hoarse as her vision began to blur around the edges through her gathering tears.

"No? Did *Dear Ole Dad* just have a hard time find-ing a babysitter this summer, then? He couldn't find someone to take you on, so he had to get creative with his childcare options?"

Anger momentarily overrode her pain. "I do *not* need a babysitter! I'm not a little kid anymore, Maxie; I'm *twelve!* I'm *quite capable* of taking care of myself, thank you very much!"

"So, I was right the first time, then. You're just a spoiled little brat getting what spoiled little brats always get. . .*Whatever. You. Want!* Well, guess what! It's not going to work out this time, *Princess*. You see, since you had to go and *tattle* on me this morning, David no longer thinks I'm a *good influence* for you. I'm sure the first thing he did at work this morning was jump online and buy me a ticket back to Hawaii. I won't be surprised if I'm thrown on some redeye flight tonight. So sad for you. Now you have to say bye-bye to your shiny new toy. Maybe *Daddy Dearest*'ll get you another one if you ask really nice."

"I wasn't *tattling* on you this morning! I was *con-cerned* for your well-being! Guess I shouldn't have worried, though, since you *clearly* don't have a care in the world for me!" Sarah spun and stomped up the stairs, afraid if she stayed a moment longer he'd see her cry, which would totally contradict not being a little kid anymore.

Shutting herself in her room and throwing herself on her bed, she went perfectly still, staring at her ceiling, reeling in shock over the drastic turn of events over the past twenty-four hours. *Here I am, alone again. Diva even stayed downstairs with Maxie. The traitor! Ugh, how did this happen? How could Maxie think such horrible things about me? Was a loving family who has time to spend with me too much to ask for? What did I do wrong? How do I fix this?! Is it too late? Will Maxie be sent back to Hawaii tonight? Did I just lose my only chance to have a brother? Do I really want one anyway, if he can hurt me as much as he just did?* Questions spun faster and faster through her mind until her sobs broke through. She rolled to her side and curled into a ball, devastated. Tears poured from her eyes, soaking pages in the book she hadn't set aside before collapsing onto the bed.

Eventually she paused, her head throbbing, eyes and throat burning. She propped herself on her elbow and began to shove her book out of her way. The sight before her stopped her cold. The words on the page were moving! No. It had to be that they were simply blurring. Sarah rubbed her eyes as if to wipe away faulty vision. Uttering a huff of disbelief, she sat bolt upright, taking the book onto her lap for a more thorough inspection. Unbelievable as it was, she had been right—the words were *physically moving* across the page! She would have screamed, but the shock had her breath caught in her throat.

The words appeared to be forming a shape on the page. Many circled until Sarah was certain they depicted the shape of a person's head. Could she believe her eyes? Had she lost her mind under all her stress and anxiety? Had she fallen asleep? Was this all a dream—?

"Sheesh, kid; breathe, already!" The words were spoken quite clearly by the woman's image portrayed on the page, complete with a head shake and eye roll of annoyance. "The last thing I need is you passing out on me!"

Sarah was too stunned to worry any further about her sanity or logical explanations. "Who are you?" she blurted out instead.

"I'm Athena. Remember? You read about me last night before bed," was the response, as if perfectly obvious.

"From the story about you and your half-brother, Ares?"

"Yes. And I don't have a lot of time here, so buck up, buttercup; we have some work to do! And for Zeus's sake, get yourself a tissue before you get snot all over me!"

"Ummm. . .okay. Uh. . .wha—what do we have to do?" Sarah asked, reaching for a tissue.

"We need to get *my* stupid brother to leave *your* brother alone before yours does something he'll regret."

"Maxie?"

"Keep up, girl! Now listen. We don't have a lot of time."

"What do you mean? I don't understand. What does Ares have to do with Maxie?"

The inked version of the goddess sighed deeply. "Okay. You've been reading this book, yes?"

Sarah nodded.

"So, tell me what you know of me and Ares."

"Um. Okay. Well, Ares is the god of war and you are the goddess of war *and wisdom.* Zeus is father to both of you, but. . ." Sarah felt a little uncomfortable voicing this part, "you're his favorite. As a matter of fact—" Sarah cleared her throat. "Ares isn't exactly Mr. Popularity among *any* of the gods. . .or humans, for that matter. You're pretty much the favorite for everyone. . .everyone except Ares. . .and *possibly* Aphrodite, since she and Ares kinda have a thing going on."

"Yes, well, if he'd stop making messes for me to clean up, I'd be more than happy to butt out of his life."

"I'm sorry, I don't understand—" Sarah huffed out a laugh. "Well, there's so much I don't understand. A biggie is that I don't understand how I'm talking to you right now! Was Ares involved with Maxie attacking Towa for no reason last night? Did Ares appear to Maxie in some book or something like you are with me now?"

"No, that would be ridiculous. That would involve forethought and planning. Ares is all about barreling in and riling up trouble wherever he can, then relishing in the unrest and battles that ensue. He favors impersonating a human to achieve his goals. Sometimes he takes on the role of an actual military leader. He's particularly proud of his stint as Genghis Khan. It took me ages to finally put a stop to him playing that character! Over the years, though, he grew bored *leading* man into battle. He now prefers to influence people to do his bidding for him. The more the peace-loving and gentle-natured the people involved, the greater the thrill for Ares when he successfully turns them against one another."

"Well. . .why Maxie? Why here?"

"Ares has been wreaking havoc all over the Middle East for years now. According to my intel, he was searching out a quiet corner of the world to vacation for a few months. Where better than the great Pacific Northwest? It took me a few days to track him down, but now we're going to put a stop to his antics before he does any serious damage."

"Yes! If it'll help Maxie, I want to help in any way I can! What do I need to do?"

"Simply speaking, there are a few essential elements to a peaceful society. Respect, of course, is the main ingredient. Then there's what I call The Three C's of Civilization. Communication. Compromise. Common ground. Ares works to break down these fundamental components of peace. We need to restore them.

"Now, if I were to just step in and stop Ares—something I'm completely capable of doing, by the way—it'd just rile him up and encourage him to fight harder for conflict, chaos and—ultimately—violence. However, if his 'playthings' regain their better judgement and refuse to act out the way he wishes, Ares will move on. There's a catch, though. Experience has taught me that—just like my efforts to thwart my brother's plans—all interventions are best made anonymously. The people involved need to feel the breakthroughs are their own. If you simply step in to solve the discourse for them, it will likely be either completely unsuccessful or it will lead to only short-term success. Following me so far?"

"I think so. Maxie needs to be reminded of the importance of communication, compromise, and common ground, but I can't let him know I'm helping him."

"Excellent! You're a quick study. . .my kind of girl! Okay. I have to go. A few major hot spots in China have my dear brother's name written all over them. I need to focus my attention there before we end up with another catastrophe. Can I count on you to put this fire out?"

"Absolutely!" Sarah was completely pumped to take on the challenge.

"All right, then. No more of those tears; they're not going to accomplish anything! Get out there and make a difference, soldier! I'll check back in when I can."

With that, the words on the page returned to their original order, and the goddess of war and wisdom was gone.

CHAPTER VII

Sarah

Sarah slumped back against her pillow, her mind reeling with ideas on how to help Maxie. Her ultimate goal was to convince him to stay with her for the entire summer. Even if he decided to fly back to Hawaii early, though, she wanted him to leave on a good note so he might consider future visits. That meant she had to make sure things were good between Dad and Maxie. She looked at her alarm clock next to her bed—she had about an hour left to plan before Dad would be home from work.

Her phone chimed with a new text. Rolling her eyes and sighing heavily, dread settling in her stomach, she grabbed her phone, assuming it was more gossip and speculation from her teammates in the group chats. She hoped not to see more cruel and hurtful words about Maxie. Part of her wanted to start a huge group chat and defend her brother. This crazy violence wasn't him; it was Ares! Maxie couldn't be blamed for being under the influence of the god of war, right? Then she laughed out loud at the responses she'd probably get if she went through with it. A van would probably come to cart her off to a mental hospital.

It wasn't a group text that had come through, though; it was a direct text from Adele.

Text from Adele to Sarah: Hey. I'm still pretty peeved @ your brother 4 attacking Towa yesterday, but out of respect 4 my friendship w/ u, I thought I should let u know. I overheard Towa talking w/ a friend of his. He plans 2 go 2 the pool @ the end of the day tomorrow & ambush Max on his way out of work. Just FYI

Sarah: Oh NO! TY so much 4 telling me! I'm going 2 talk 2 Maxie tonight 2 find out what happened last night. I'll get back 2 u as soon as I find out more

Great; another level of difficulty. Now Maxie was either being shipped off on a plane tonight or getting pummeled after work tomorrow. Assuming Maxie was still in Washington tomorrow, she could warn him about the ambush, but that would probably just lead to more violence.

She'd have to find another way to prevent the showdown.

*   *   *

"Hi, Daddy! How was your day?" Sarah greeted the moment Dad walked into the kitchen from the garage.

"Pretty good, kiddo. My meeting went really well this morning. How was your day?"

"Ummm. . .interesting, I guess."

"Oh yeah? What made it so interesting?"

Oh, you know, Sarah thought, *a vigilante gymnastics team out for the blood of my brother who has fallen victim to the god of war, making it necessary for me to team up with the goddess of war and wisdom to sort it all out . . . typical stuff, really. Yeah; that explanation won't fly. Gonna have to go with something a little more pedestrian.* "Uh. . .Lucky had some new toys that she and Div really went nuts over."

"Oh good," Dad commented distractedly as he sifted through the mail.

"I hope you don't mind; I ordered Chinese food for dinner. I knew you and Mom would probably be tired after a long day at work. It'll be here any second. I remembered the pot stickers you like, too."

"Oh, nice!" Dad smiled, the subject of food bringing his full attention back to Sarah. "We'll have to set some aside in the microwave for Mom, though. I just got a text from her that she's going to be late. Where's Max?"

"He's downstairs in the screen room. Oh—and there's the delivery guy," Sarah announced as the doorbell rang. "If you get the door and sign the slip, I'll get Maxie and meet you in the dining room."

Minutes later the three of them were seated at the table and Diva was content on her bed in the corner, chewing on the bone Sarah had gotten her. Now Sarah just needed to make sure Dad and Maxie got through dinner just as contentedly as her dog.

"Max, I apologize for blowing up the way I did this morning," Dad offered as they served themselves from the takeout boxes. "I was wrong to jump to conclusions, and I should have offered you the opportunity to explain."

"Okay." Maxie looked surprised by Dad's admission, relieved but wary he might be falling for some sort of trap.

Dad continued calmly. "Would you like to tell me what happened last night?"

"Yeah. Sure." Maxie cleared his throat. "My buddy Aaron pointed out a guy who was around the kids Sarah was hanging out with. He said the dude had been—" He shot a glance at Sarah. "Uh. . .disrespectful with some of the girls. He told me to make sure he didn't bother Sarah and her friends. Later I saw one of the girls pushing that guy away and yelling at him. All I could think of was getting him away from her."

Sarah was about to blurt out that Towa would never do such a thing, and nobody had complained about him at the beach, but that particular comment wouldn't help Maxie at all. Instead, she filed the information away to investigate later. And Aaron. . .Maxie had mentioned Aaron before. She needed to find out more about that guy.

Dad took a deep breath and shook his head. "Well. . .you see? It was wrong that I didn't give you a chance to speak this morning and—even more unacceptable—assumed the worst. I said we don't condone violence in our house, and we don't. But obviously, if you are protecting someone, that's a different situation. Well done, Max. Well done."

Maxie nodded, looking pleased. Sarah breathed a little easier, feeling things were headed in the right direction. They were still on some shaky ground, though. Communication—this was a good time for more communication.

"Daddy, Maxie told me a little about his mom the other day—that she's a yoga and hula instructor. Will you please tell me more about the time you spent with her?"

Dad paused for a moment, a smile crossing his face, his eyes taking on a dreamy look. "I met Kalani almost immediately after being stationed at Wheeler Army Airfield. I had never been to Oʻahu, and I was completely blown away by the beauty—of the island *and* the woman."

Sarah snuck a peek at Maxie as Dad relived his memories. From the rapt expression on his face, it appeared he had never heard this before.

Dad continued. "The base had a luau to welcome my unit to the island, and Kalani was one of the hula dancers. She was incredible. It was like she was Hawaii personified. She was the warmth of the sun, the rhythm of the waves, and the beauty of the hibiscus flower. I was completely smitten. Then she was kind enough to speak with me after her dance, and I fell even harder for her warm, fun-loving and carefree nature.

"We spent as much time together as we could over the next few months. I met her wonderful family, and she introduced me to the rest of the island. It was just. . .a magical time." Dad paused again, lost in his memories, and cleared his throat. "Then life interrupted, as it is often wont to do." He shrugged and took another bite of his fried rice.

"Well, what happened?!" Sarah prompted, unwilling to let go of the fairytale. She knew how it ended, of course—with Dad moving to Washington and meeting Mom and being 'the luckiest man alive to find true love twice,' as he always put it, but she had never heard the details between the two tales.

Maxie continued to watch Dad intently.

"My unit was called up," Dad explained, his voice now flat and emotionless, "for deployment to the Middle East."

Sarah knew Dad had been in the military, but he never spoke about his time overseas. She leaned forward, soaking in every new detail.

Dad nervously fidgeted with his fork and knife. "I did a year tour in Afghanistan." He paused, then cleared his throat again. "Kalani and her family sent care packages that helped the time go by a little easier. She wrote occasionally, but she mainly just sent amusing anecdotes that were probably meant to offer me a reason to smile—which I was thankful for. There weren't many reasons to smile over there. She wasn't one for very serious letter-writing, but that was fine. I was just so anxious to get back home to her!"

He paused again, long enough this time that Sarah wondered if he would continue at all. Maxie sat quietly, waiting.

"We were actually just weeks from coming back when—" He took a deep breath. "When a bomb meant for our convoy exploded in front of us. We were *lucky,*" he said, adding the air quotes. "I wasn't hurt too bad—just a concussion and some broken bones. Unfortunately, the same can't be said for. . .for the poor Afghani civilians who happened to be on the bus in front of us." Dad shook his head slowly, closing his eyes and rubbing his forehead. He took another deep breath and pushed on with his tale.

"Instead of me coming straight back to the states as planned, my injuries forced me to spend a few months in Germany for treatment and rehab. I finally got back to O'ahu nearly a year and a half after leaving. Kalani was as beautiful as ever." Smiling now, Dad chuckled. "And imagine my surprise when I was introduced to my nearly one-year-old son!"

"Wait, you met me?" Maxie asked.

"Wait, you didn't *know* you had a son?" Sarah asked at the same time.

Dad laughed. "No, I didn't know. Kalani apparently learned she was pregnant at the same time I got my deployment orders. She didn't want me to worry, so she didn't tell me. She never wrote a single word about it in her letters. And yes, Max, I met you. You were an *adorable* baby, and I fell in love all over again the minute I saw you."

"Why'd you leave, then?" Max demanded.

"Well, now, that's where things got complicated," Dad began. He pushed his plate aside. "My unit had returned to the island well ahead of me, of course, during my unplanned trip. Soon after I got there, we got transfer orders to Joint Base Lewis McChord here in Washington. Kalani and I had planned to marry, but this move made us stop and think about our future. Max, you know Hawaii is your mother's life. It's what she does, where she belongs. . .it's who she is! I couldn't ask her to leave the home and family she so loved. And of course, I had no way to refuse the transfer orders, either. I was stuck between a rock and a hard place.

"To make matters worse, I was. . ." Dad looked up to the ceiling. "I was finding that my physical injuries weren't the only ones I had left Afghanistan with," he admitted quietly. "I was suffering pretty bad from PTSD, and hearing horror stories about other soldiers, I worried about what type of husband and father I could ever be. Your mother and I decided that we would go our separate ways—at least for the short term. I had been sending money to Kalani from the time I left for Afghanistan. I continued to support you both financially, of course. Your mom, grandparents, uncles, and all the rest of your extended family was just much better suited to offer you the loving upbringing you very much deserved."

"Oh, the account," Maxie mused quietly, nodding his head.

Dad and Sarah looked at him with raised eyebrows.

Maxie explained, "Well, money has never seemed like an issue for us, but then again, we've never really needed much of anything, either, aside from a new surfboard from time to time. I'd like to go to school for oceanic environmental science, so one day last winter Makuahine told me I have a savings account with more than enough money for whatever school or major I decide."

"Well, even if she hadn't saved that money for you, I would certainly make sure you get whatever education you desire. Max, please don't ever interpret my lack of involvement as a lack of interest or love for you. I know I should have reached out to you a long time before now. It's my biggest regret. It's just. . . When you were young, I was afraid you'd be confused. . .and. . .I don't even know where the time went! Before I knew it, you were older, and I. . .I felt like I had waited too long. I thought I lost my chance to have a relationship with you."

Dad shot Sarah a warm smile before continuing. "But then Sarah came to my rescue, calling me out on being the idiot I've been all these years."

"Oh, Dadddyyy." Sarah stood up and rounded the table toward him. She hugged him from behind his chair and kissed the top of his head. "You know I'll *always* be here to call you an idiot!"

She then skipped up the stairs with Diva in tow to give Dad and her brother some alone time and to start brainstorming the next phase of *Operation*

Save Maxie. After closing her bedroom door and getting situated on her bed, her first instinct was to call Keelie. She still had too many unanswered questions, though, and Adele was the person who could probably answer at least a few of them.

Text to Adele from Sarah: I've got my tweed coat, magnifying glass, pipe, and funny hat. I'm ready for a serious game of real-life Clue. 🕵 ?4U What was Towa doing just before Maxie attacked him last night?

Adele: BRB

Adele: He said he was putting ice cubes down the back of Hannah's bathing suit. 😊

Sarah: Y did he do that?

Adele: Hold on

Adele: He said she had filled his sneakers w/ wet sand

Sarah: sec

Text to Hannah from Sarah: Did u put wet sand in Towa's shoes yesterday?

Hannah: Yeah

Sarah: Oh. Y?

Hannah: He threw my towel in the water

Sarah: Oh. BRB

Text to Adele from Sarah: Did Towa throw Hannah's towel in the water?

Adele: w8

Adele: Yeah, cuz she buried his sunglasses in the sand

Adele: He also said "What's with the friggin' 20 ?'s, get out of my room!" 😠 so I hope u have the info you need, cuz I don't know if he'll answer any more

Sarah: K. Hold on

Text to Hannah from Sarah: Did u bury Towa's sunglasses in the sand?

Hannah: Negatory

Hannah: Y the heck would I do that?!

Sarah: Yeah; that'd just be silly! 😜

Text to Adele from Sarah: Y'd Towa think Hannah buried his sunglasses? She said she didn't do it

Sarah: & I swear; I think that's the last ?

Adele: ugh. . .sec

Adele: His buddy Aaron said he saw Hannah do it

Sarah: SHUT. UP!

Sarah: Aaron?! Dude, Aaron is Maxie's "friend". Last night HE'S the 1 who told Maxie 2 keep an eye on Towa cuz Towa was acting hella creepy w/ girls! ☺

Adele: Whaaaa??? That's stupid. Towa isn't creepy with girls! Mom would totally kill him if he was!

Sarah: I know that & u know that, but MAXIE wouldn't know that

Adele: & Aaron is the guy who Towa told about his plans 2 get his revenge on Max. If Aaron is Max's friend...WTH??? 😵

Sarah: I know, right?! K. . .we need to stop our brothers from killing each other tomorrow. Gotta make a plan. BRB

Text to Keelie from Sarah: Found out what happened yesterday w/ Maxie & Towa. Turns out they were punk'd. Now they're gonna kill each other tomorrow afternoon if we don't find a way to stop it. Ideas?

Keelie: Just tell them

Sarah had thought of that, of course, but then she remembered back to Athena's warning about Maxie knowing she was responsible for solving the situation. Communication, compromise, and common ground, she had said. . .

Text to Keele from Sarah: Something tells me that won't work. Long story; don't ask. Can u look Towa up on Facebook, Twitter, Instagram, and SnapChat 4 me? What's he like? What's he into?

Keelie: Sec

Keelie: Uh. . .seriously into video games

Keelie: Not a huge fan of school

Keelie: Loves whales

Keelie: Into skateboarding

Sarah: Wait; what about whales? Y did u say he loves whales?

Keelie: He has a bunch of links 2 news reports & petitions 2 save an Orca pod in the Puget Sound. . . About that mom Orca who carried her dead calf around w/ her for a few weeks last summer (so sad!!!), how pod members are dying of starvation, how noise pollution in the H2O is a big problem 4 them, yada, yada. Y?

Sarah: I think that might help.

Keelie: Orcas dying will help keep Maxie & Towa from pummeling each other? ☺

Sarah: Maxie's really into marine life, 2

Keelie: If u say so. . .

Sarah: I think I have a plan. B4N ♡

Keelie: c ya!

Text to Adele from Sarah: Is Towa into orcas?

Adele: Geez. . .random much?

Adele: & yeah, actually; he wants 2 get into marine biology or something & he's really into activism about the local orca pod

Sarah: Perfect. Got a plan.

Adele: & ur just gonna leave me hangin' on what whales have to do with anything?

Sarah: 😏 Yep. But I'm gonna text u a note "from Maxie" that you'll need 2 show Towa 1st thing in the AM

Sarah: & when u see it it'll make sense

Adele: Kk. . .if u say so

Sarah: Oh, & I'm also gonna email u a note "from Towa" that I want u 2 copy/paste & text back 2 me 4 me 2 show Maxie 1st thing in the AM

Adele: Got it

Sarah: Awesome. Thx! ttut

Sarah grabbed a notebook and pen off her desk and set about drafting perfect notes for the guys to send one another. An hour later, after multiple revisions, she was happy, so she sent the first off to Adele.

Text to Adele from Sarah: Hi Adele! Maxie wanted to contact Towa, but he doesn't have his # & neither do I. Plz let Towa read this msg from Maxie in the AM. Thx! ☺

Sarah: Towa, my name is Max. I want 2 apologize for starting that fight w/ u yesterday @ the beach. I've learned we were duped by my buddy Aaron (well, FOR-MER buddy Aaron). He told me u were harassing girls & said to watch u cuz u have a bad rep 4 hurting girls. I saw that girl scream & hit u & I lost it. Sorry, dude; I shouldn't have listened to Aaron. I'd actually like 2 talk sometime, tho. I hear ur really into saving ocean life. R there any groups around here that do beach clean ups or anything? I want 2 help if I can. BTW, my # is 808-555-8988

Email to Adele from Sarah: Here's the text I want you to send to me "for Towa". Please add his phone number at the end. Thanks so much; you're the best!!! ☺

Max, this is Towa. I planned on confronting u today about what u did @ the beach. I have found out, tho, that the whole thing was schemed out by my buddy Aaron (actually, FORMER buddy Aaron). He made it look like I was attacking my friend Hannah (which I totally wasn't; we were just joking around; u can ask her) & then I guess he encouraged u to "save her from me". I don't blame u, since this is all Aaron's fault. I'd like 2 get together, tho. I hear ur really into saving ocean life. I'm fighting hard 4 our local orca pod. Maybe u'd be interested in helping out? My # is

Hopeful that her plan would work, Sarah settled into bed with Diva and her Greek mythology book, focusing on stories about Ares. She was sure Aaron must really be the god of war. She didn't want to think of what would happen if Ares got his way and transformed Maxie into some sort of troublemaker.

CHAPTER VIII

Max

"**M**orning, Maxie!" Sarah called from her bedroom door, as if lying in wait for Max to open his.

"Morning," he grumbled.

"Hey, I got this text for you last night." Sarah swiped at her phone's screen and started walking toward him.

"What do you mean I got a text?"

"Towa wanted to get in touch with you, but he doesn't know your number, so he got my number from Adele."

"Who?" It was too early for so much to follow.

"Towa—he's the guy you pummeled the other day—"

"Let me see!" He grabbed Sarah's phone. Was Mr. Handsy coming clean about his unacceptable behavior? Was he taunting Max before trying to catch him unaware later?

Max read through the message, shook his head, and rubbed a hand over his forehead, not knowing what to make of the words. His mind raced. *This says ". . .my buddy Aaron. . .!" Aaron is friends with the guy he told me is a sexist jerk? Does this message play into Towa's plan for revenge? That doesn't seem right; he even admitted he had planned to jump me. He actually sounds like a cool dude. Why would Aaron do this?*

Grabbing his phone, Max typed in Towa's number and shot off a text.

Text to Towa from Max: Dude, I can't believe Aaron. What an ass! We totally need to let him know what he did was NOT COOL! And saving orcas? Yeah, I'm totally down w/ that; what can I do 2 help?

Towa: I have a plan to get back at Aaron. Call me; we'll discuss payback & orcas.

*   *   *

"Hey, mister?"

Max looked down from the lifeguard chair to find a little freckled red-haired kid solemnly looking up at him.

"So, like, um. . .you kicked my friend Luke out of the pool the other day? But, like. . .he didn't do anything wrong. He said *you* said he was pushing me under the water, but that's not true." Freckles threw in an adamant shake of his head for emphasis. "I was seeing if I could lift him up on my shoulders, just like he lifted me up."

Oh. . .so this was Green Trunks's victim. "Hey, buddy. Sorry if I misinterpreted what was happening right then, but your friend had been dunking kids all afternoon, and sometimes if you misbehave over and over, you get in trouble, even if you aren't truly misbehaving at that given moment."

"Nu-uh, he wasn't dunking kids," Freckles spat. "I was with him the whole time. . .until you kicked him out." He threw in a glare to ensure Max knew what he thought of Max's actions. "If he was dunking kids I wudda saw it, and I didn't see nothin'!"

"Okaaay." Max drew out the word slowly, considering how to respond. "Thank you for the update, buddy. I'll make sure I apologize to your friend."

That was apparently the right answer for Freckles, because he offered a single head nod and walked off.

Max huffed out a little disgusted laugh and shook his head, mentally adding Green Trunks to the list of poor, unsuspecting victims of Aaron's reckless manipulation.

*   *   *

"Hey, man, thanks again for the head's up about this afternoon." Max clapped Aaron on the shoulder as they prepared to leave the locker room at the end of the day.

"You ready for this guy?" Aaron smiled, his hunger for a big fight obvious.

"More than you could imagine. Come on. I can't wait to give him exactly what he deserves!"

Sarah

"Shhh. . .here they come!" Sarah whisper-yelled.

Emmie and Keelie crowded in closer for a better look around the lilac bush they were hiding behind.

"Wait—" Emmie hissed. "I thought you said Towa and Max worked everything out this morning! They're circling each other like two gunslingers from The Wild West. The only thing we're missing is a tumbleweed blowing across the parking lot and the soundtrack to *The Good, the Bad and the Ugly*!"

"Do-do-do. . .wha, wha, whaa. . .do-do-do. . .wha, wha, *whaa!*" Keelie whisper-sang the tune of the classic western movie.

Sarah was too stressed to appreciate their joking. "I thought they *did* work it all out!" She panicked. Had she misread Maxie's calm, relieved nature after reading the text from "Towa?" She even heard him call Towa later in the morning. Why would they chat if they were still planning to fight?!

Sarah wrung her hands, petrified that she had completely failed her mission. She had told Athena she was *on* this, that she had it handled! Maybe she *was* too young to take on such an important operation, because this was shaping up to be a failure of epic proportions.

"What should we do, Sar? Should we go out there and stop them?" Keelie wondered.

"I don't *know!*" Sarah bit her knuckles.

Maxie and Towa stopped their circling, and with ferocious battle cries, they charged one another.

Sarah turned away, unable to witness the violence, feeling like a coward but still incapable of facing it. She held her breath, anticipating the sickening thud of colliding bodies she remembered all too well from the other night at the beach.

Instead, the yells transformed into exuberant exclamations of welcome. Sarah turned back in time to catch Maxie and Towa doing the man hug thing where they embrace with one arm and slap each other on the back with the other. She wanted to laugh in relief—and cry—but all she could do was collapse, too emotionally exhausted for anything else.

She jumped at the roar of an extremely angry voice. It wasn't Maxie's or Towa's voice, though; it was Aaron. He. Was. *LIVID!*

Emmie giggled. "Somebody seems ticked that he didn't get the MMA fight he thought he had bought himself."

Keelie chuckled along. "Awww. . .poor baby."

"Sorry, man," Maxie yelled at Aaron, "we're not your *puppets!*"

"Yeah," Towa chimed in. "You can't just try to make people lash out at each other like that! Why would you do it, anyway?! That's messed up, dude!"

"Total waste of my time!" Aaron yelled in disgust, throwing his arms up in the air and shaking his head as he stormed over to his big black truck.

Maxie and Towa laughed and waved goodbye.

The girls cheered and shared a high-five.

CHAPTER IX

Sarah

"Sit rep?"

"Wait. . .what?" Sarah asked.

The face on the page sighed impatiently. "Situation report," Athena clarified slowly.

"Oh! Uh. . .all good, I think!" Sarah smiled proudly. "Nobody is planning any more fights that I know of, least of all Maxie because now he and Towa are working together to coordinate a beach clean-up where they'll also be protesting the heavy boat traffic that affects a local whale pod. Ares took off in a major huff. I don't even want to think about the mood he'll be in tomorrow at the pool!

"Excellent. Don't worry about Ares; you won't be seeing him again. When things don't go his way, he immediately moves on to another locale. My intel is that he's already in South America," Athena explained. "But this has been a particularly good outcome," she added, "because not only did you prevent further violence, you went above and beyond and facilitated a partnership for a good cause. The more energy people transfer toward positive goals, the less capacity they have for intolerance, hate and aggression. You did very well here, Sarah. Thank you. I truly appreciate your help."

"Anytime! I'm just so glad I could help Maxie. I was worried I would lose him, and so soon after finally getting to meet him, too!"

"I must be off to thwart my brother's next scheme. *You* need to go knock some sense into *your* brother, though! Make sure that boy understands the danger in attacking others only on the advice or opinions of someone else. If you're going to go to the extremes of violence, you have to make that judgment for *yourself*; you can't be manipulated into it."

"Okay," Sarah agreed solemnly.

Then Athena's voice seemed to soften. "After that, enjoy your time with your brother. He's a good kid." She smiled, then she was gone again, the book having reverted back to just words on a page.

Sarah took a deep, satisfied breath as she petted Diva, then she left her room, searching for Maxie. Not surprisingly, she found him in the screen room, playing Fortnite.

"Hey," she greeted as she sat down.

"Hey," he greeted back distractedly.

"I'm glad you worked everything out with Towa today," Sarah offered.

"Me, too; he's pretty cool."

"So, the whole reason you fought him in the first place was because of something that Aaron guy told you?"

"Yeah. . .stupid, huh?"

"Well, I can see trusting the word of your friend," Sarah sympathized, "but decisions about other people—good or bad, right or wrong. . .it seems like those should be based on more than what someone else tells you."

"No, you're right. I was a total idiot for not getting any evidence first. I won't be doing that again!" Maxie shook his head for emphasis.

"Good," Sarah said sincerely, "because I love you and would hate for you to ever get hurt again!"

Maxie shot her a quick but warm smile.

Sarah quietly watched him play his game for a few minutes, then broke the silence. "Maxie, what was that you called your mom last night?"

"*Makuahine*. It just means 'mom' in Hawaiian."

"It's beautiful. Can you teach me some other Hawaiian words?"

"Hmmm. . .sure. Uh. . .There are actually five words in Hawaiian that kinda make up who we are and what we're all about. One is *Ohana*—family. That doesn't just refer to the people you live with or people you share blood with, either. In Hawaii it's everyone; we're all 'cousins'; we're all here for one another."

"Oh, *Ohana*. . .I remember that from *Lilo & Stitch*."

Maxie smiled. "*Pono* is another very important word."

Sarah tried the word out. "*Pono*."

Maxie nodded his approval. "It basically means doing the right thing. The more you live in harmony with pono, the happier you are. And there's *mana*. That has to do with the power each of us has to be successful—but not in the sense of being rich or famous—successful in finding meaning in your life. *Pono* helps to gain *mana*, you see?"

"Oh, I get it! That's so cool! Okay, so *ohana*, *pono*, and *mana*."

"Right. Then there's one you've heard before—*aloha*. People use it as a greeting, but it goes deeper than that. It's all about the beauty in life—in everyone and everything we see and do. And, of course, there's *aina*—that means land. In Hawaii we spend most of our lives outdoors, so we're really conscious of the connection we have with the environment and the importance of taking care of it."

"Oh, right. That's why you're so passionate about the pollution in the ocean."

"Sure, but it's concern for *all* of our planet. Like, in my house we use solar power for our electricity. Then we have a small electric car, we keep a garden, we recycle and compost. . ."

"My friend Mylee was talking about composting the other day. She's in a gardening club, and they've been working on getting the community to compost more."

"That's cool. Maybe you can join the club with her. Gardening is really fun, and it would give you more people to do things with when your parents are working."

"I hadn't thought of that! That would be good, actually. I love my family and all, but. . .they're really busy a lot and it can get lonely sometimes," Sarah admitted quietly.

Maxie shot a look over at Sarah before returning to his game. "You know, I'm really sorry for blowing up at you the way I did yesterday. I wasn't acting like myself. You're not a spoiled brat. I see how much time you spend alone here. I mean, you've gotta feel *pretty* lonely to dress in matching outfits with a dog," he teased.

"Shut up!" Sarah laughed. "My matchy outfits with Diva are *awesome!*"

"If you say so!" Maxie laughed.

Sarah sat back and thought on all Athena and Maxie had said today. "This is all so inspiring," she thought out loud.

"What is?"

"Mylee with her gardening and composting, Towa with his efforts to save the whales. . . Yesterday when I was talking to Keelie about you working to clean up the oceans, I even learned that Emmie volunteers a few days a week to help non-English speaking kids at the preschool."

"Man," Maxie exclaimed, shaking his head. "Beautiful, fun *and kind*; I really need to get to know this girl better!"

"I know, right?!" Sarah stopped to think for a minute. "What if. . ." she ventured, slowly, "what if we all had a place to chat about all this, all the—what did you call it? *Pono?*"

Maxie nodded.

"I mean. . . If we had a place where everyone could learn about all these great things we're doing, I bet we could inspire more to join in, just like I'm feeling inspired now!"

"You might be on to something there."

"Keelie is the tech guru—I'll see what she thinks would work best. We could make some sort of chat room where people share the cool things they're doing to help people or the environment. And maybe more people will start working together, too, like you and Towa are now."

"That actually sounds like an incredible idea, Sarah."

"Oo. . .we could call it *Club Pono*." Sarah clapped excitedly, her idea taking off in her head.

"Sounds awesome." Maxie smiled.

"I'm gonna go call Keelie. . .and Mylee to ask about the gardening club!" Sarah sped up the stairs to her room.

*   *   *

"This is so much fun, Maxie; I never in a million years would have thought I could drag Mom and Dad out for a night of dinner and bowling—and in the middle of the week, even!" Sarah gushed as she watched Dad line up for a hopeful strike.

"Yeah," Maxie agreed with a smile. "You need to convince them to do this on a regular basis. Sometimes adults get lost in their work unless they plan to step away every so often."

"I'm definitely going to ask Daddy if we can do this, like, every other week or something." Sarah nodded. Then she held her breath and finally blurted out the question she had been wanting to ask for days. "Are you having enough fun to want to stay with us for the summer?"

Maxie paused before answering, making Sarah nervous. "I was all over the place when I first came here," Maxie finally began. "Emotionally, that is. I felt so lost. The whole situation seemed so crazy, and I didn't know how to respond. So, I guess I kinda just. . .ran through a whole bunch of different responses, trying to find the right one. All that got me was frustrated and starting to feel mad, which I didn't like. I was anxious to leave because I thought I'd be leaving behind those bad feelings, you know?"

Maxie looked over at Dad, who was doing a ridiculous touchdown dance and trash-talking Mom, who was lining up for her next shot. "But that talk with David—with Dad. . ." He seemed to be trying out the word. "That talk with Dad the other night, learning about when I was born. . ." Maxie stopped for a moment, deep in thought. "That made all the difference. I thought at first that I wouldn't want to have any type of heart-to-heart because it might make things feel worse. I feel a *connection* now, though. I want to learn more about him. And I'm liking that

I'm getting to know you better, too. You're a pretty cool kid, Sarah." He smiled. "And I guess I actually have you to thank for it all, right?"

Sarah shyly looked down at her hands. "I'm so glad you came and I'm so, so, *so* glad you're staying! Life is so much better with you here."

"You know, when I do go back home, we can keep in touch. You have Skype, right?"

Sarah sucked in a quick breath as she realized what Maxie was saying. "I hadn't even thought of that!" She smiled excitedly.

"And maybe we can even convince Dad and Rebecca for you guys to come out to the island for Christmas or something. I could teach you how to surf."

"Ohmy*God*, that would be So *Awesome!*" Sarah screeched. She was about to throw her arms around him for a huge hug, but pulled back at the last minute, remembering Maxie's non-hugger tendencies.

Max smiled at her, spread his arms wide and said, "Come on, half-pint. Bring it in!"

Sarah launched herself into his arms. "Ahhh..." she sighed as she melted into his embrace.

Maxie rubbed the top of her head, laughing when she demanded he stop messing up her hair, then pulled away to fetch his ball and take his shot.

Sarah dropped into a chair and breathed in deep. She felt so full—so full of love for her family and hope for her future.

Today was a *great* day, and she just *knew* her days ahead would be even better!

ABOUT THE AUTHOR

Ellie Collins

Ellie Collins wrote her debut novel, *Daisy, Bold & Beautiful* when she was turning eleven and just beginning sixth grade. She finished writing *Mylee in the Mirror*, the second in her multi-award-winning middle grade Greek mythology series before heading back to school for seventh grade and turning twelve and *Mad Max & Sweet Sarah* before eighth grade and becoming a teen. She writes amid a very busy extra-curricular schedule, including a spot on both a gymnastics team and a trampoline and tumbling team, as well as taking weekly piano lessons. She's an avid gamer who loves hanging out with friends. Her love of Greek mythology inspires her writing.

https://authorelliecollins.wixsite.com/mysite
https://www.instagram.com/authorelliecollins/

Fresh Ink Group

Publishing
Free Memberships
Share & Read Free Stories, Essays, Articles
Free-Story Newsletter
Writing Contests

❦

Books
E-books
Amazon Bookstore

❦

Authors
Editors
Artists
Professionals
Publishing Services
Publisher Resources

❦

Members' Websites
Members' Blogs
Social Media

Twitter: @FreshInkGroup
Google+: Fresh Ink Group
Facebook.com/FreshInkGroup
LinkedIn: Fresh Ink Group
About.me/FreshInkGroup
FreshInkGroup.com

Also by Ellie Collins!

D.J. and her dad moved far from the small town and only home she ever knew. Now she's starting middle school in the city with kids she's never met. She tries to make friends, but they all appear to be slaves to screen time. D.J. just likes to garden, nurturing plants, watching them grow and thrive. It seems she'll never find a way to fit in, but then she awakens in a gorgeous garden where she meets Persephone, Goddess of Spring. She must be dreaming; her new friend can't possibly be real—and what could she know about getting along with gamers? D.J. really needs some ideas, or she might never find her own place in a complicated world.

GREEK MYTHOLODY SERIES

Young-adult novels by Ellie Collins

First three books